ANCIENT HISS STORY

LEIGHANN DOBBS

ALSO BY LEIGHANN DOBBS

KATE DIAMOND
Adventure/Suspense Series

Hidden Agemda

MYSTIC NOTCH
Cat Cozy Mystery Series

Ghostly Paws
A Spirited Tail
A Mew To A Kill

BLACKMOORE SISTERS
Cozy Mystery Series

Dead Wrong
Dead & Buried
Dead Tide
Buried Secrets
Deadly Intentions
A Grave Mistake

LEXY BAKER
Cozy Mystery Series

Lexy Baker Cozy Mystery Series
Boxed Set Vol 1 (Books 1-4)

Or buy the books separately:

Killer Cupcakes
Dying For Danish
Murder, Money and Marzipan
3 Bodies and a Biscotti
Brownies, Bodies & Bad Guys
Bake, Battle & Roll
Wedded Blintz
Scones, Skulls & Scams
Ice Cream Murder
Mummified Meringues
Brutal Brulee (Novella)

DOBBS "FANCYTALES"
Regency Romance Fairytales Series

Something In Red
Snow White and the Seven Rogues
Dancing On Glass
The Beast of Edenmaine
The Reluctant Princess
Sleeping Heiress

CONTEMPORARY ROMANCE

Sweet Escapes
Reluctant Romance

ANCIENT HISS STORY

CHAPTER ONE

Kate Diamond stared at the oil painting on the table in front of her and wondered why her boss wanted it so badly. Sure, it was old. Very old. But she couldn't see what made it special enough to warrant sending someone all the way from the *Ritzholdt Museum* in Boston to East Overshoe, Ohio, in order to acquire it. Couldn't they have just wired the money and had the owner ship it?

Not that she was complaining. She'd have done just about anything to get out of the stifling boredom of the *Ritzholdt Museum*'s security office where her job as chief security liaison had consisted of shuffling papers around her desk for the past three months. She found the desk work boring, but thankfully that was only a small part of her job. Normally, she was assigned to the more important field work of retrieving stolen artwork and relics.

There hadn't been any field work for several months,

which seemed odd because there was always something going on in the museum world. But if there had been field work, she would've known about it seeing as she was chief security liaison. And there was no reason for her boss not to send her out in the field. Well, not unless he was worried about her freezing up like she'd done in Stockholm.

Kate pushed away her uneasy feelings about the Stockholm incident and told herself that it had been no big deal. She'd been sent out to retrieve an important religious artifact and had ended up in a gunfight. That in itself wasn't unusual and Kate was a pretty good shot, but the problem was she'd frozen up right in the middle of things and almost gotten herself and her partner killed.

Luckily, she'd only frozen for a few seconds and it had ended up okay. They'd secured the artifact and Kate and her partner had been fine, other than a small scar on Kate's arm where she'd been grazed by a bullet.

It wasn't being shot that had bothered her the most. It was the battery of tests that the museum had thrust on her to determine if she was suited for field work. That, and her wounded pride.

The tests had proven she was fine. She'd merely had a moment of intense anxiety under high stress. It could happen to anyone. She'd been cleared to go back in the field months ago and apparently, this was the first field work that had come up.

She'd jumped at the chance to fly out to acquire the painting. True, this was about as exciting as watching bowling in comparison to some of her other assignments, but it sure beat shuffling papers.

She looked up from the painting to the senior citizen seated across the Formica table from her. Estelle Perkins, the owner of the painting, fretted with the frayed hem of her avocado and gold pineapple-patterned apron. The apron looked to have been purchased around 1975 and apparently Estelle didn't think she'd needed a new one since then, preferring to make this one last as evidenced by the careful stitching indicating minor repairs in several spots.

Looking around the kitchen, Kate noticed the appliances and furnishings were decades old. Estelle must have applied the same philosophy to everything she owned.

Estelle seemed like a nice woman. Frugal. Salt of the earth type. Kate didn't want to lowball her, but she also didn't want to pay too much. Besides, the amount she was about to offer would probably seem like winning the lottery to an elderly person on Social Security.

"So, fifty thousand, then?" She'd been advised to pay up to two hundred and fifty thousand, but having seen it in person, she hardly thought the painting worth it. Maybe Max had made a mistake or this was the wrong painting. At the very least, she could save the museum some money and make some brownie points while she was at it.

Estelle's mouth tightened. Her eyes drifted over to door. "Well, I don't know…" Estelle shifted in her seat and looked down at the painting again. "I think it's worth more than that. There seems to be a bit of interest in it."

Interest? Kate's boss, Maximilian Forbes, hadn't said anything about anyone else being interested in the painting. Kate got a funny feeling in the pit of her stomach which was validated by the knock coming from Estelle's front door.

Estelle bolted up from her seat. "My, my, who could that be?"

She shot Kate and apologetic look and bustled off toward the front. Kate's nerves started to work overtime.

Estelle came back with two strange men who looked just as surprised at Kate's presence as she was at theirs. The men wore almost identical black suits and had almost identical short buzz haircuts and dark sunglasses. One of them had an onion-shaped black mole on his face. Kate was fleetingly reminded of the movie, *Men in Black*, but these guys looked more like thugs than aliens.

"What is this?" Onion Mole gestured toward Kate.

"Well…" Estelle seemed flustered, and with good reason. She'd snookered both of them, playing Kate and the *Ritzholdt Museum* against the *Men in Black*—whoever they were. It was a dangerous game, but Kate could kind of understand where the old lady was coming from—she just wanted to get the most she could for the painting.

"Kate here is from the *Ritzholdt Museum* and I was just telling her how much interest this little painting had garnered. I was very confused about who to sell it to and I wanted to make sure you all saw it before purchasing it." Estelle looked around uncertainly. "That's why I invited you all here to look at it."

Onion Mole scrutinized Kate. "*Ritzhold Museum*? What do *you* want with it?"

Kate shrugged. Neither man made an attempt at hand-shaking, so she didn't, either. But she felt at a disadvantage not knowing who the *Men in Black* represented. "Oh, you know, we like to buy paintings to hang up around the museum. Spruces the place up … and who might you be?"

The men ignored her question. Onion Mole looked down at the painting on the table. "Is this it?"

Estelle nodded.

The two suits bent over the painting. Kate noticed that one of them, the man without the mole, had a gold serpent ring on his finger. Its ruby eyes winked at her and made her shudder. Kate did not like snakes.

The *Men in Black* finished their inspection, looked at each other and nodded.

"We will buy it," Onion Mole said.

"Hey, wait a minute," Kate cut in. "I'm going to buy it."

Snake Ring glanced at her as if she were insignificant. "I do not think so. We have come here specifically to acquire the painting."

Kate bristled. "Yeah, so have I."

He ignored her and turned to Estelle. "How much?"

Estelle glanced from Snake Ring to Onion Mole to Kate. Her finger worried a thread on her apron while she considered his question. "My late husband, Frank, bought this painting at the estate sale of the archaeologist, Reginald White. Frank always said it had value beyond its subject—whatever that means. He was very good with antiques, you know. Anyway, he always told me that the best way to figure out what an antique was worth was to let the market decide and so I think we should let the market decide."

Onion Mole scrunched up his face. "What does that mean?"

"You people should bid on it. I'd like to get as much as I can and it seems the only fair way." Estelle gestured around the kitchen. "As you can see, Social Security only gets you so far."

"What?" Kate stared at Estelle incredulously. She didn't like the idea of bidding against these guys, but she had to admit she had a newfound respect for the old lady who had pulled this trick off to get as much as she could for the painting. Now she'd probably have to pay the full two hundred and fifty thousand that Max had allotted but she felt kind of glad it was going to Estelle. What the heck. It wasn't her money, anyway.

"It's the only way to establish fair market value. You guys are lucky I wasn't able to find more bidders." Estelle picked up a copper teakettle from the top of her bulky, white 1940s stove. "Tea, anyone?"

"We don't want tea. We will pay one hundred thousand dollars," Onion Mole said.

Kate straightened in her chair. Fine. If that was the way they wanted it, she'd play. "One hundred fifty thousand."

Onion Mole glared at her. "One seventy-five."

"Two hundred," Kate shot back.

Onion Mole darted a look at Snake Ring. Snake ring nodded. Kate figured they must be getting maxed out.

"Two twenty-five," Onion Mole said.

Shoot, it was getting close. But Kate would be damned if she'd let these guys waltz in and steal the painting right out from under her.

"Two fifty." Kate leaned back in her chair and crossed her arms over her chest smugly. Given the look they'd exchanged fifty thousand dollars ago, she was sure they wouldn't want to pay more than that for the painting.

"Three hundred thousand," Onion Mole shot back.

Crap! Kate's eyes drifted from Snake Ring to Onion Mole to Estelle. Estelle was still standing at the stove, a tea kettle in one hand and a yellow gingham towel in the other. She was staring at them with rapt attention. Probably already spending the money.

Kate was only supposed to go up to two fifty, but the museum was loaded with money and with Estelle being the payee, she felt like it was going to a good cause. She wasn't cleared to make the decision to spend more, but she knew Max really wanted the painting and she couldn't very well call him and ask for permission right in the middle of bidding. Plus, if these guys were so gung-ho to pay more for it, it obviously must be some sort of a find. Max would be upset if she didn't go all out to secure the painting for the Ritzhold and it ended up in some other museum.

"Five hundred thousand!" Kate smiled disarmingly at Onion Mole.

Onion Mole's brow creased but with those dark glasses on, it was impossible to read his eyes. "Fine, have it your way."

The feeling of triumph that surged through Kate's chest was short-lived when he pulled the strangest-looking gun she'd ever seen out of his jacket. It looked like some sort of modern day blunderbuss. Kate would have been intrigued if he wasn't pointing it at her face.

"I see you will not back down, so I regret that we will end the bidding here," Onion Mole said.

Snake Ring piped up. "Wally, the boss said not to kill—"

"Shut up!"

Kate squeezed her eyes shut and wondered how badly it hurt to have your face blown off as she heard the click of the hammer.

She was surprised to find out that it didn't hurt as bad as she would have thought. She expected an explosion of pain in the front of her face, but instead, it was more like a sting in the side of her neck.

Her knees went weak and her eyes flew open as she collapsed on the floor. Across the room, Estelle stared at Onion Mole with wide eyes as he swung the blunderbuss in her direction.

Kate wondered how she could even still be watching what was going on. Maybe she was having one of those out-of-body experiences she heard people had when they died.

Onion Mole squeezed off a shot and a dart flew out of the gun. It zoomed toward Estelle's foot, stuck into her big toe and vibrated back and forth like a javelin.

A dart gun!

As if in slow motion, Kate watched the teakettle fall to the floor, bouncing once as water splashed out. The tea towel fluttered onto the top of the stove as Estelle slumped to the floor.

Kate's fingers flew up to her neck and felt a similar dart. Her face hadn't been blown off! She'd just been stuck with a dart. That may or may not have been preferable, considering whatever was on the dart had turned her legs into useless logs, rendered her arms barely able to move and was now causing her vision to fade.

As Kate lost the battle for consciousness, the last thing she saw was the *Men in Black* scoop the painting off the kitchen table on their way out.

CHAPTER TWO

Kate jerked awake. Opening one eye, she saw a big, bunion-afflicted toe with a dart sticking out of it and quickly remembered why she was lying on the floor. Then her heart kicked in her chest as she noticed the smoke.

Estelle's house was on fire!

She pushed herself up. The adrenaline that was now shooting through her veins cleared her head quickly and washed away the residual effects of whatever was on the dart she'd been shot with.

A quick glance over to the stove told her what the problem was. The stove top and wall behind it were on fire. Kate remembered the tea towel Estelle had been holding when she got shot with the dart. She must have dropped it on the gas stove and it caught on fire.

Estelle was in a heap at the foot of the stove. Kate

hurried over, touching her hand which, thankfully, was warm.

"Estelle! Wake up, the house is on fire!"

She pulled the dart out of Estelle's toe. And then the one out of her own neck.

"Ouch!" Estelle scowled at her. "What happened?"

"Those men in suits. They knocked us out and took the painting."

"Darn it!" Estelle's face crumpled. "I was counting on the money from that for my retirement. Social Security doesn't even pay the taxes on this place anymore."

Kate pulled the old woman up. "We have more important things to worry about. Your kitchen is burning."

"Oh, is that what that smell is? I just thought the stove was on the fritz again."

Kate's heart hammered in her chest as she pulled Estelle to her feet. The flames were spreading quickly—what did Estelle have on her walls? Kerosene?

The faded chicken and basket motif wallpaper curled off the wall in strips as the flames spread onto the suspended ceiling. Kate knew they had to get out of there fast before the ceiling fell in. Estelle, on the other hand was taking her sweet time.

"Come on, we'd better get out of here!" Kate yelled, trying to instill some urgency in the senior citizen.

Estelle held her hand up. "Okay, okay. I guess I never should've gotten fancy trying to have an auction on that painting. I should have just sold it to you." She glanced at the kitchen table and her brows shot up to her forehead. "Well, looky there."

Kate looked at the table. The painting was gone, but

in its place was a pile of money.

The *Men in Black* had left money?

What were they, some kind of gentlemen thugs? She stood there staring at the table wondering how much money they'd left. Was it their top bid of three hundred grand or their initial bid? What did a hundred grand even look like? Kate had no idea.

While Kate stood looking, Estelle had already high-tailed it to the hall closet and pulled out a duffel bag. She bustled back to the table and started shoving the money inside.

A flaming ceiling tile fell down behind Estelle. The woman must have had nerves of steel.

"I don't know if we have time for that, Estelle!" Kate tugged on Estelle's elbow.

Estelle pushed her away. "Phooey. I didn't go through all this to just let this money go up in smoke!"

Estelle shoved the rest of the money in the bag and Kate pulled her out of the kitchen into the living room, then shoved her through the front door and took off across the yard. Estelle took one wistful backward glance before following Kate.

From outside, Kate could see the kitchen end of the house was now engulfed in flames. Lucky thing she'd woken up when she had. She scrambled as far from the house as she could. Estelle, clutching the duffel bag to her chest, followed her to the edge of the road, where they collapsed on a log.

"Who were those guys?" Estelle asked.

"You're asking me?" Kate said. "You're the one that invited them. How did you find them?"

"Actually, they found me." Estelle frowned. "As I seem to recall, they'd recently heard that Nelson—that's my husband—had the painting in his possession. I had already contacted the *Ritzholdt Museum* and you were already on your way here, so I figured if I scheduled them to come out on the same day, I could get you into a bidding war."

"Yeah, that ended up good." Kate had a hollow feeling in the pit of her stomach. Something told her there was more to this painting than met the eye.

Estelle grimaced, then looked at the bag. "Well, at least I got something." She glanced back at the burning house. "Should we call 911?"

Kate was already dialing 911 on her phone, though she was more interested in finding out who the men were. What kinds of art buyers carried dart guns and shot their clients and whoever else was in the room when the bidding didn't go their way? Clearly, something more than just art was at stake here, but it didn't seem like Estelle knew much more about the *Men in Black*.

She made the call, then stared at the cell phone in her hand, her stomach sinking when she realized she'd have to call the *Ritzholdt* and report what happened. Clearly, there was more to this painting than Max had let on. Either he didn't know or he'd kept that information from her, but either way she'd failed on her assignment and she didn't relish the thought of telling him.   On the other hand, she hadn't frozen in the face of danger. She'd gotten her and Estelle out of the burning house. At least that was something.

Crash!

14

Behind them, the roof in the back of house caved in. Kate realized her own problems paled in comparison to Estelle's. The woman had just lost her house.

Kate put her hand on Estelle's arm. "You going to be okay?"

Estelle shrugged. "Yeah, sure. It has been kind of a long, weird day. But I think I'll be okay."

Kate's heart crunched. Maybe Estelle didn't realize the magnitude of what was happening behind them. "But your house is burning down. Everything's destroyed."

Estelle glanced back at the house. She gave an easy-come, easy-go half-shrug and patted the duffel bag. "That's okay. It was time for me to buy new stuff anyway."

CHAPTER THREE

But *why* did those guys want the painting so bad?" Gideon Crenshaw, chief scientist at the *Ritzholdt Museum*, asked early the next morning after Kate had told him the whole story in full detail.

They were sitting in Gideon's lab which encompassed most of the basement of the museum. Some of the lab real estate was dedicated to preserving and restoring paintings and artifacts, as one might expect in the basement of a museum. But what most people wouldn't expect was that the bulk of the lab was reserved for Gideon's gadgets and experiments.

Sometimes those experiments had to do with making solvents and cleaners for artifact restoration, but most of the time, they had to do with creating gizmos, tools and concoctions that would help Kate in her job of retrieving items stolen from the museum.

Naturally, being a museum, the *Ritzholdt* had billions of dollars' worth of items, and naturally those items were often the target of thieves. Not so much while they were on display in the museum, but during the acquisition process or when the items were being loaned out to other museums and private parties.

Of course, the museum reported these thefts to the police, but the police were usually swamped with high priority crimes and that's where Kate came in. She would be sent off to 'retrieve' the stolen items by whatever means possible.

Sometimes she had to use unorthodox methods and that's where Gideon's gadgets, concoctions and tools, along with Kate's training as a former FBI agent, came in handy.

When there were no stolen objects to track down, Kate helped procure items for the museum's vast collections, which was what she had been doing out in Ohio. That was usually a pretty safe job, so she normally didn't arm herself. However, given what had happened at Estelle's, Kate made a mental note to take a trip to Gideon's lab the next time she went on an acquisition trip.

"I was hoping *you* would know why it was so special. It looked just like a regular painting to me. It wasn't even that good," Kate said.

"I don't know … unless…" Gideon's green eyes squinted shut behind eyeglass lenses as thick as coke bottle bottoms.

"Unless what?"

"I'm not sure. Max didn't say anything to me about it being unusual and I don't want to speculate. We'll have to see what he says."

"We should ask him. I know there's more to this painting than meets the eye," Kate said.

"No point in asking him. You know how he is. He's tight-lipped. If there is something and we need to know, I'm sure he'll tell us." Gideon twisted his lips together. "The whole thing is rather strange, though. Why didn't they just come in and take it from you in the first place?"

Kate shrugged. "I'm not sure. I got the impression they had orders to try to buy it like normal."

"Probably, so as not to arouse suspicions."

"Yeah, well, I don't know about that. Shooting us with poison darts would tend to raise eyebrows."

Gideon's forehead creased in concern and he looked at Kate's neck. "But it sounded like they only did that as a last resort, after you insisted on outbidding them. I wonder what was on those darts."

"I have no idea. Whatever it was made my muscles go weak and then knocked me out. I don't know how long I was out, but when I woke up I don't remember feeling that bad. Although I was kind of preoccupied with not burning up in the house fire so maybe I just didn't notice."

"Those symptoms sound almost like a synthetic de-rivative of snake venom," Gideon said.

Kate thought about the ruby-eyed serpent ring. "Snake venom? Do you really think they would get ven-om from a reptile and put it on the darts?"

"I didn't say it *was* snake venom. I said a synthetic derivative that causes similar symptoms. I use a formula of it for some of our serums."

Kate remembered an assignment not long ago where Gideon had outfitted her with a modified perfume vile that actually injected a serum into her victim. The serum had knocked him out for hours so Kate could rifle through his computer for information. The victim woke up unharmed, but unable to remember what had happened. She supposed it would be hypocritical to get worked up about the *Men in Black* for using a similar serum on her.

"I wonder why they left money?" Gideon asked.

"Maybe they actually had a conscience. I remember Snake Ring saying the boss told them not to kill anyone right before Onion Mole shot me."

"But then they left you to burn in the fire … I mean, how would they know that you would get out in time?"

"I don't think they knew the place was on fire. They ran out the door with the painting right after they shot us with the darts. The towel probably hadn't caught fire yet and you wouldn't have been able to see the flames from outside the house for quite some time. They were probably long gone by then."

Gideon nodded. "If their boss told them not to kill anyone, that means someone is behind this. I mean, other than the two thugs. They were just minions … just like Max suspected."

Kate's left brow ticked up a notch. She'd had to leave a voice message on Max's cell phone with the bad news. She'd been a little nervous about his reaction as he hadn't yet called her back. One reason she'd come to work early was that she was hoping he might come down to see her about it in person.

Gideon knew that it was an ongoing source of frustration for Kate that, despite having worked for Max for almost two years, she'd never actually seen him. She'd talked to him plenty of times on the phone, through Skype, over texts, but she'd never seen his face. And she was dying to find out if his looks matched his sexy, smooth baritone voice.

The lab door whooshed open and Kate twirled her chair, thinking this might finally be the big moment. Who else would be here this early besides Max? But the excitement that bubbled up in her chest fizzled out when she saw it was only Max's assistant, Mercedes LaChance.

Mercedes fixed Kate with a scowl which Kate enthusiastically returned. The two women didn't get along. In fact, Kate had a sneaking suspicion that Mercedes took great glee in keeping Kate from ever meeting Max in person. Not only that, but she was a pain in the butt about expense reports.

Mercedes' doe-brown eyes drifted over to Gideon and her lips cracked in a smile. Ever fashionable, she wore a tailored navy suit with white piping. Her glossy, brown hair was piled up on top of her head in a stylish up-do that made Kate unconsciously run a hand through her unruly, copper curls.

Kate noticed Mercedes was holding a cell phone out in front of her as if she had someone on speakerphone.

"Max…" Mercedes chirped into the phone.

"Yes, Mercy, did you find them?" Max's deep voice, edged with an Irish—or was it English—accent and laced with concern came from the phone.

"Yes, I found them both in the lab. I'm there now and

I have you on Facetime."

"Kate! I've been trying to call you and let you know I got your message," Max said.

Kate's eyes darted to her own cell phone. Max had been trying to call? She swiped her phone off the table and pressed the button. Dead battery.

"Hi, Max. Sorry, my cell phone's dead." Kate grimaced.

Mercedes smirked and held her phone at an angle so Kate couldn't see Max.

"That's okay. I wanted to be sure to reach you to let you know that I thought you did a wonderful job despite the fact that you were unable to secure the painting," Max said.

Kate got up from her chair and walked over to stand next to Mercedes. She was taller than the petite brunette and hoped to be able to easily get a glimpse of Max on the phone's display over Mercedes' shoulder. "Thank you, Max. I'm sorry I wasn't able to get the painting, but under the circumstances, it was impossible."

Just as Kate got to Mercedes shoulder, the other woman turned so they were facing each other. Mercedes held the phone up straight, smiling at the display and leaving Kate staring at the back of the phone.

"I certainly hope that you were not harmed?"

Kate warmed at the genuine concern in Max's voice. "I'm fine. Wasn't hurt at all." She craned her neck forward to look over the top edge of the phone. Seeing Max upside down would be better than nothing.

Mercedes snatched the phone away, holding it higher. "She looks fine to me, Max."

"Good. Good. It wouldn't do for you to get hurt, Kate. I would be very upset and I'm terribly sorry to put you in harm's way."

Kate shuffled to the side a fraction of an inch. If she moved slowly, maybe Mercedes wouldn't notice her sidling over to get a glimpse. "Oh, no problem. I always manage to land on my feet. I did survive the FBI, after all."

Max chuckled. "And Mrs. Perkins? Is she okay? I hope her house was not too damaged."

Kate took another quarter-inch step to the side. Mercedes wasn't paying attention. She was busy making eyes in Gideon's direction. Kate shot a look over her shoulder at Gideon. What was up with that? Was he making eyes back?

"Kate?"

"Oh, sorry, Max. Estelle wasn't hurt. Her home was a total loss but she didn't seem to mind. It turns out the police deemed it an accident. She'd dropped the tea towel when she got shot with the dart and that started the fire, so she told them the truth except the part about the bad guys, the dart and the money on the table. The insurance company is going to pay her a hefty sum and the men that took the painting left a lot of money, so she actually ended up with quite a windfall. To tell you the truth, she seemed pretty happy about the whole thing. Said she was going to buy a retirement condo someplace in Florida."

"Those men exhibited rather odd behavior, wouldn't you say?" Max's voice asked from the phone.

"We were just talking about that," Gideon said as Kate made another sidestep. Just one more step and she'd be able to see the display.

"Could you describe the men to me?" Max asked.

As Kate started to describe the *Men in Black*, Daisy, Gideon's Dachshund, who typically spent the bulk of her day leisurely napping in the lab, suddenly realized there were people present and came trotting out from one of the rooms that housed one of Gideon's many secret experiments.

Mercedes' eyes lit up and she fell to her knees to pet the dog. Unfortunately, the phone went with her and was now facing the floor, making it impossible for Kate to see the display.

"Did the mole look like an onion?" Max asked.

Kate exchanged a look with Gideon. "Yes, it did! Do you know who it is?"

"Unfortunately, I do." Max's deep voice was laced with concern. "Those men work for Igor Markovic of the *Lowenstaff Museum*. He's been a thorn in my side since day one."

"That's right," Gideon said. "I know he's tried to beat us out of quite a few artifacts."

"True." Max's voice was muffled because Mercedes was so busy petting Daisy, she had the phone pushed against the dog's fur. "He plays dirty and I simply cannot tolerate that."

Kate tapped Mercedes on the shoulder and made hand-over-the-phone motions. Mercedes scowled, cradled the phone protectively against her chest and stood up.

"Yeah, that's right. We can't let him just waltz in and take stuff from us at gunpoint!" Gideon was saying.

"Or dart point…" Kate added.

Gideon's face turned thoughtful. "But what can we do about it now?"

Max sighed. "The museum game can be a tough one. There's a lot of competition for the best items. People use creative methods to acquire them, but even so, there has to be some level of fairness. People can't just run off half-cocked, pulling guns and burning down houses to get what they want. As far as I'm concerned, Markovic cheated. He stole that painting right out from under us using unfair methods, and I think there is only one thing we can do now to vindicate ourselves and make it right."

"What's that?" Kate asked.

"Steal it back."

CHAPTER FOUR

K ate never did get to see Max on Mercedes' phone. He'd hung up too quickly, claiming not to want to know the details and leaving it all up to Gideon. Naturally, stealing the painting back required a lot of planning and a little bit of deception, which was why Kate found herself in Florida, sitting in a Toyota Corolla rental car outside *Golden Capers* the next afternoon. Inside the nondescript retirement community lived people who were the best she knew when it came to deception and stealing—her parents.

Kate got out of her car, taking note of the quiet. That was good. It meant the usual raucous party wasn't in progress. Parties happened often at *Golden Capers* and it didn't matter what time of night or day. Apparently, retirees had to have something to keep them occupied. She opened the fence around the pool and stepped inside.

Sunlight winked off the surface of the aqua blue, in-ground pool. In one corner of the fenced-in patio area, a chrome blender gleamed on the counter of a grass tiki hut. Colorful paper lantern lights dangled from the top of the hut. A bikini top floated in the pool and Kate tried not to think about how it had gotten there.

Most of the lounge chairs surrounding the pool were empty except for two across the pool, each of which held a wrinkly senior citizen. One of them waved at Kate enthusiastically.

"Kate! Your mom said you were coming. We can't wait to get started!" Gertie Rosenbloom slouched in the lounge chair. Her oversized, rhinestone-studded sunglasses competed with the pool for most likely to blind someone with glare. Beside her, Sal Munch shot Kate a greeting with his eyebrows over the top of his newspaper and then went back to reading.

Gertie and Sal were friends of her parents and fellow residents at *Golden Capers Retirement Community*.

Well, perhaps 'friends' and 'residents' weren't exactly the right words. Come to think of it, 'retirement community' might be a little misleading, too.

Gertie and Sal, like all the other people that lived at *Golden Capers*, including Kate's parents, were former thieves. The senior citizen swindlers were long-since retired … or so they claimed. While *Golden Capers* resembled any other retirement community on the outside with stucco buildings, a pool, tennis courts and Wednesday night pot luck dinners, what most people never suspected was it was entirely filled with ex-thieves and con men. Not just your garden variety, either—the real pros in the field. The ones that had been wildly successful and retired *before* they got caught.

Everyone at *Golden Capers* had known each other 'back in the day'. They'd worked on jobs together and when it came time, pooled their money to buy the community outright where they all lived like one big family. This way, they could talk freely about old times and practice their skills without anyone getting suspicious.

Kate didn't know how, but somehow Max had known about Kate's association with the *Golden Capers* crew. Sometimes, she wondered if that might have been one of the reasons he'd hired her, because he often suggested she enlist their aid in her 'assignments'.

Not that the gang minded—they lived for it. It was a great way for them to stay in practice and relatively 'safe', seeing as Max could usually use his pull to get them out of any minor problems with the law. For the most part, no one bothered notifying 'the law' about any of the heists Kate and the crew pulled off because they were usually retrieving items that had been stolen from the *Ritzholdt Museum* in the first place.

Kate waved to the two sunbathers and then skirted the pool on her way to the steps that led to her parents' condo. *Golden Capers* wasn't lavish, although she was pretty sure they could've afforded something a little more upscale. They probably just didn't want to draw attention to themselves. It was a very simple complex, with Lemon Bay behind the units and the Gulf of Mexico across the street. All in all, not a bad gig.

Her parents had a large unit on the second floor. The door swung open as soon as she tapped and there stood her mother. Carlotta Diamond looked twenty years younger than her age of sixty-eight. She was petite, with thick chestnut hair that hung to her shoulders. The thin strands of silver that highlighted the hair at her temples only served to give her an air of sophistication that matched her slight European accent. Her brown, almond-shaped eyes crinkled at the edges in a smile for her only daughter.

"Honey! So good to see you!"

Kate bent down to hug her mother, who was a good foot shorter than her. The scent of Chanel Number Five conjured up happy childhood memories as the two women embraced affectionately.

Despite being brought up by a jewel thief mother and con artist father, Kate had had a relatively normal childhood. She'd done everything other kids had done and her parents had acted the same as other parents. Okay, it was a little strange that she had this large entourage of aunts and uncles who weren't actually related to her, but her parents had done everything they could to keep her life normal.

She'd never suspected that her parents and extended family were a little bit unusual until she'd gotten older. In the meantime, her 'aunts' and 'uncles' had taught her a variety of unique skills, like lock-picking, disguises and pick-pocketing—all of which were coming in handy now, given her choice of career.

"Kitten!" Vic Diamond waved from the lanai at the opposite end of the condo.

"I have snacks outside." Carlotta led Kate through the condo, which was apportioned with the finest money could buy, with upscale kitchen cabinets, granite countertops, Carrera marble flooring. But the best part about the condo was the view. In the back was an un-obscured view of Lemon Bay—a large expanse of water dotted with mangrove and palm trees. From their second story perch, they could watch boats sailing past on their way to the channel that lead to the Gulf of Mexico. Tropical birds flitted in the trees and even an occasional dolphin graced the bay with its appearance.

The mild breeze ruffled Kate's hair as she followed her mother through the sliding glass doors.

"Did you have a nice trip?" Vic asked.

Kate kissed her father on the cheek before sinking into a cushioned patio chair in between her mother and father. "The flight was kind of bumpy, but overall it was good."

Kate studied Vic. His short-cropped, salt-and-pepper hair—mostly salt now—gave him a distinguished air. Even though he was almost seventy, his face was relatively free from lines. His golden tan was a testament to his active, outdoors lifestyle as was his sturdy build. His ready smile, which showed off his perfect teeth and the gleam in his eye, all added to his youthful appearance.

Kate felt blessed that both her parents were in good health and enjoyed an active lifestyle. That lifestyle probably helped keep them looking so young. That and good genes. Kate hoped she'd inherited the looking-young-for-your-age gene from them.

"That's good. We're so glad to have you here." Vic slid the laptop that was open in front of him over so Kate could see the screen. "I was just talking to Gideon here on Skype."

Kate waved to Gideon, whose face took up most of the screen. "Hi, Gid."

"Hey, Kate. Your Dad and I were just discussing the painting."

"Okay. Anything new?" Kate had told her parents the whole story about what had happened at Estelle's when she'd called the day before to ask for their help. While she'd been packing and flying down, Gideon had probably done more research and he and Vic must have been well into making plans. Kate would need to catch up.

"It seems that Max has someone on the inside at the *Lowenstaff Museum* and he got word that the painting is there," Gideon said.

"They have it on display already?"

"No, not on display. It's in the basement. Max's contact didn't know exactly why, but I assume it would be for restoration. Do you remember if the painting needed work?"

Kate wrinkled her forehead, trying to remember what the painting had looked like. She wished she'd looked at it closer, but at the time, she thought it would just be an easy acquisition. Hindsight was always twenty-twenty. "It did look pretty old. I guess it might have needed some repair."

Vic slid the laptop back in front of him. "I'm running some scenarios through the software now. We'll know more about the best way to retrieve it in a minute."

Vic referenced the special 'heist' software that one of their computer expert friends had created. Vic had assured Kate they only had it created to use for practice, as a video game of sorts. Apparently, it got pretty boring having parties out by the pool all the time, so the *Golden Capers* gang liked to practice their old skills even if they didn't put them to practical use anymore. The software was part of that, but it turned out that it also came in handy for some of Kate's assignments.

"I sent over some blueprints of the museum layout in case you need them," Gideon was saying.

"Thanks, kid," Vic replied. "We might need some of your other unique talents once we get the plan worked out."

"No problem. Anything you guys need. Oh, and Kate…"

"Yes?"

"Max wants to make sure that you leave money for the painting. He said that we're not thieves. We don't steal things, and since the painting wasn't technically stolen from us and Markovic paid Estelle for it, we need to pay for it, too. Otherwise, we're no better than he is."

"Okay," Kate said uncertainly. She didn't really think leaving money was necessary. As far she could tell, the whole stealing business when it came to this painting was walking a fine line anyway.

"So I'll send that down along with whatever equipment you guys need."

"Sounds good." Kate remembered the pile of money on Estelle's kitchen table and wondered how they would lug around a big duffel bag full of money while they were trying to pull off a museum heist. She assumed it would be cash since they couldn't very well leave a check.

"This is going to be so exciting." Carlotta's eyes sparkled.

"Gee, Mom, you're acting like we're going on a fun vacation. We *are* breaking in and stealing something," Kate pointed out.

"I know. That's what makes it exciting."

Carlotta had been one of the best jewel thieves in the business. She'd broken into countless homes and other places. That's how she'd met Vic. When they combined both of their skills, they were unstoppable.

But Kate's parents hadn't just used their skills to accumulate money for themselves. They'd done good things with their skills, too. Things like retrieving items stolen by governments during various wars and giving them back to their rightful owners.

Sure, they took a little bit of payment for themselves along the way, but just like the others at *Golden Capers*, they'd never hurt another human being. It was a special code with all the *Golden Capers* gang who had rarely brought guns on any of their jobs.

"What's so special about this painting, anyway?" Vic asked.

Kate shrugged. "I'm not sure. It was pretty old. But I got the impression that getting it back from Markovic was a matter of pride with Max. They have a long-standing rivalry."

Vic's eyes narrowed. "Seems like this is going a bit far for it to be a matter of pride. There has to be more."

"I'm sure if there was more, Max would have told me." Wouldn't he? Her father had a point. It *was* going a bit overboard. The thought that Max might not trust her enough to tell her made her chest tighten.

Vic and Carlotta exchanged a glance.

"Maybe he's trying to keep you safe," Carlotta suggested. "You know, the less you know about it, the better. You know how bosses are. They don't always want to tell all their secrets. Makes them feel important."

Kate's chest constricted another notch more because of what her mother *hadn't* said than her actual words.

"Oh, I see. You guys think Max didn't tell me because he was afraid I would freeze up again. Is that it?" Kate hated the defensive tone that had crept into her voice.

Carlotta patted her arm. "Of course not, dear. Everyone freezes up once in a while. It's very common, especially in high stress situations. It's happened to me countless times." Carlotta shot a glance over to Vic.

Vic chimed in, "Me, too."

Kate narrowed her eyes at her parents. Were they just telling her that to make her feel better? She'd never known them to lie to her, even for her own good. Somehow, the thought that her parents weren't perfect, either, mollified her.

She relaxed back into her chair. Her mother was right, of course. But that still didn't explain why Max's interest in the painting was a little bit over the top.

"Did you get a good look at the painting? Who was the artist?" Vic asked. "Maybe we can have Sylvia do some research." Sylvia was another of the *Golden Capers* gang who had specialized in art.

Kate sighed. "I guess I should have paid more attention to it, but I honestly thought it was just a routine

35

pickup. It was old, but it wasn't even by anyone famous, or at least not that I could tell. The signature was just a scribble."

Vic's face screwed up in thought. He was just about to say something else when the computer dinged, stealing his attention.

"Aha! This is perfect." Vic's eyes shone as he looked over the top of the computer screen at them. "The *Lowenstaff* is having a big event to show off their new Faberge egg exhibit this Friday. There should be thousands of extra people milling around and lots of chaos going on … a perfect opportunity for us to use as camouflage while we steal the painting."

CHAPTER FIVE

Vic zipped off assignments to the others via email, then got to planning. They scheduled a meeting out by the pool at five p.m.

"What the heck," Vic said. "Might as well combine it with happy hour."

Carlotta got busy outlining her part of the heist, alternating between that and making her famous seven-layer dip.

At five p.m. sharp, they gathered around the pool. Gertie decorated a long table with a plastic pink flamingo tablecloth and everyone put a dish on it. There were deviled eggs, curried carrots, finger sandwiches, meatballs and brownies. It looked more like a potluck supper than a meeting on how to steal a painting from one of the country's largest museums.

Inside the grass tiki bar in the corner, Sal had the

blender on high, whipping up a batch of margaritas and pina coladas. He used the Swiss army knife-like gadgets hidden in his prosthetic thumb—courtesy of Gideon—to open the cans of coconut milk.

They sipped umbrella drinks, nibbled the food and made small talk while sitting on the patio loungers and around the small, glass-topped umbrella tables. At six o'clock, Vic clapped his hands.

"Okay, everyone, let's get down to business." He sat down at one of the tables with his laptop and they all milled around him, some standing with drinks in hand, others pulling their chairs over.

"As you all know, we've been commissioned by the *Ritzholdt* to help … umm … acquire a painting from their rival museum, the *Lowenstaff.*"

"'Bout time. It's been kind of boring around here," Frankie said.

"Yeah, and we could always use some more money to line the coffers," Sylvia joked.

"But we'd help our Katie for free, right?" Sal asked.

"Yes!" everyone chorused and Kate's heart warmed at her extended family's willingness to help even for free, although she'd long suspected that their eagerness to help on her assignments had more to do with the excitement than the money.

"Anyway," Vic continued. "The *Lowenstaff* is having a gala event to show off their Fabergé egg exhibit and we'll use that as our cover."

Sylvia elbowed Carlotta in the ribs. "Fabergé eggs? I bet you'd like to get your hands on one of those."

"But she wouldn't do that, would she?" Vic leveled a look at Carlotta.

"Of course not," Carlotta bristled. "I'm out of that business now."

"How will we get in?" Benny asked. Benny was an expert on security systems. Kate knew he would be chomping at the bit, hoping this would give him an opportunity to ply his skills. "I hear they have a pretty sophisticated alarm system."

"That's where this event is going to help us," Vic said. "We're going to go in as part of the cleaning crew. The painting is in the basement, presumably for restoration. With the activity of the event, we should be able to sneak down there without being noticed."

"And then what? You gonna just walk out with the painting under your arm?"

"Sort of. But not through the front door. We're going to take a lesser-known exit." Vic gestured toward Gertie, who was standing beside the tiki bar with a rolled-up paper in her hand. She moved over to one of the tables and motioned with her hand for everyone to pick up their drinks before spreading the large paper out on the table.

"This here is a blueprint of the New York City steam tunnels. No one uses them anymore. In fact, many of them were sealed off decades ago. But it just so happens that one of the working tunnels goes right to the *Lowenstaff museum*."

"Are you sure these are passable? I mean they could be filled up with water and rats and stuff," Charlie said.

"Maybe even snakes," Frankie offered.

An image of the gold snake ring with the ruby eyes surfaced and Kate shuddered at the thought of snakes.

"Me and Frankie are going out tomorrow and do some recon to figure out the best exit strategy and see if the tunnels are passable. I called one of my former contacts about them and he said the route we wanted was all clear back in ninety-nine."

"So, you don't need me to disarm any alarms or anything?" Benny's voice dipped in disappointment.

"We might," Vic said. "I need you to study up on their system, just in case. In particular, find out anything you can about the preservation area in the basement so we'll know what we are up against once we get in."

"Will do."

"I've already found out who the museum uses for cleaning. They've hired a special service for the event. Gideon will make us exact replicas of the uniforms and get us the appropriate badges. We should be able to walk right in."

"And then it will be a breeze," Carlotta added. "Because, as we all know, cleaning people are virtually invisible."

Everybody laughed at that. They'd all used the cleaning person disguise at one time or another.

"Surely, there will be guards even in the lower levels. Especially if there are artifacts and paintings being restored," Sylvia said.

"Ahh. That's where the brilliant part of my plan comes in," Vic said. "While the non-English-speaking cleaning crew is insisting on entrance to the restoration room, there's going to be a surprise visit by the New York City Board of Tunnel Inspectors."

"They have tunnel inspectors?" Bennie asked.

"No, but I doubt the guards know that," Vic replied. "I'll have official badges and a uniform."

"That stuff's easy," Charlie chuckled.

"It sure is," Vic continued. "Anyway, I'll try to distract them as long as I can so the fake cleaning ladies can grab the painting. If our blueprints are correct, the steam tunnel door opens into their lab. The tunnel doors are locked from the tunnel side but I'm sure the lock will be a piece of cake for Gertie."

"Darn tootin'," Gertie said.

"She'll open the door for us and we'll escape down the tunnel before the guards know what hit 'em." Vic looked around at the crowd. "Does anyone see anything wrong with this plan?"

"Is there any way we can get inside to that basement area ahead of time?" Sylvia asked.

Vic nodded. "Yes, I almost forgot. You're right, we do need to take a look at it ahead of time. I know that little old ladies get lost in museums all the time and find themselves in the basement when they were really just looking for the ladies room. Isn't that right, Ginny?" Vic looked at the petite woman pouring a pina colada into a large glass.

"That's right." She stuck a piece of pineapple in the drink.

Vic nodded. "I'll have Gideon send out one of those brooch cameras and Ginny can bring back pictures so we know exactly what we're dealing with, and can try to anticipate any problems as well as map out alternate escape routes."

"That sounds great," Benny said. "And I'll check out the security on the other floors, just in case you have to go out that way."

"Excellent." Vic shut his laptop. "I think that's it, then. Are there any more questions?"

"I think you pretty much covered it," Sal said, taking a noisy sip of his margarita. Then he added those famous last words that probably would have been better left unsaid. "This is gonna be the easiest job we've ever pulled off."

CHAPTER SIX

Kate couldn't believe the woman standing in front of her was her mother. The slim, fashionable Carlotta had been transformed into a frumpy old lady in a nondescript, gray cleaning uniform, complete with thick, rubber-soled shoes.

Kate, herself, was unrecognizable in a similar uniform. But it wasn't just the uniforms. Gideon had sent an array of disguise materials which, when combined with her parents' extensive selection of makeup, contact lenses and wigs, had worked magic. Kate was willing to bet that neither she nor her mother would have been recognized even by their own family members.

Kate and Carlotta each had a laminated ID card hanging from a chain around their necks, which had worked perfectly to gain them entrance to the *Lowenstaff Museum*. Once inside, they'd stuck to the back corridors and stairways so as not to disrupt the guests who were already starting to arrive for the event. No one had paid them any attention.

They knew exactly where to go thanks to Ginny, who had come out a few days before and done her old lady act, gaining access to the basement and snapping a few pictures of the area as well as bringing back information on the best route for Kate and Carlotta to follow inside the museum.

They'd made their way through the halls with their cart of cleaning equipment, taken the freight elevator to the basement and followed Ginny's directions to the restoration room, in front of which they now stood.

Kate looked into the room through the glass window and recognized the painting, which lay on a table. It had been taken out of the frame and there were brushes and solvents next to it. Apparently, someone had been working on restoring it.

Unfortunately, their access to the room was blocked by two young guards who Carlotta was jabbering at in some foreign language. Italian, maybe? Kate had no idea what the language was and, judging by the confused looks on the guards faces, neither did they.

Kate watched with amusement as her mother gestured wildly toward the door then at her cleaning cart, trying to indicate to the guards that they needed to get inside to clean.

One of the guards—Jim, his nametag said, frowned down at her. "No admitto." He thrust his arm out toward the hallway, indicating for Carlotta and Kate to leave.

Carlotta unleashed a barrage of foreign words, causing Jim's brows to rise as he exchanged uncertain looks with his coworker. They both took a step back from the crazy cleaning lady.

"Look, lady, we don't need any cleaning in here," the other guard, Brian, said. He looked over at Kate imploringly. "Don't you speak English?"

Kate just frowned at him as if she didn't know what he was saying and clutched her modified Kirby vacuum cleaner, which doubled as a container for the money Max insisted they leave after taking the painting.

Carlotta made a move toward the door, grabbing the handle and opening it slightly.

"No!" Jim shook his head, grabbing her arm and pulling her away.

The elevator behind Jim dinged, pulling his attention from Carlotta. The doors whooshed open and Vic stepped out, wearing a dark blue uniform. His facial features had been altered using putty and makeup and he sported a long, dark beard. Kate almost didn't recognize him.

Vic whipped out a badge and shoved it in Jim's face.

"Bud Kingsly, Chief Inspector, steam tunnel division," Vic barked with authority.

Jim's brow creased and he glanced at Brian. "I don't know anything about any inspection. Where did you say you were from?"

Vic drew himself up to his full, six-foot height. "Don't try that with me. You people have known about this inspection for a week. Let me into the room or I'll have to shut this place down right now. I'm sure your bosses won't like that with all those VIPs milling around upstairs."

"We didn't hear anything about any inspection." Brian looked at Jim for confirmation.

Vic walked over and opened the door. "Look, guys, it's not my problem that your bosses didn't tell you about the inspection." He held up a clipboard and tapped it with his finger. "You can see right here that the city wants me to inspect this today. I need to get this paperwork in by midnight or the museum will be in violation and you two will be responsible."

Jim chewed his bottom lip. Kate noticed he was just a kid, not much older than twenty. He glanced into the room, then shrugged. "I guess it can't hurt. What did you say you were inspecting, anyway?"

"The steam tunnel door over there." Vic pointed to the corner of the room where a gray panel was set in the wall. "Opens up to the city steam tunnels. Got to be inspected every five years to make sure you're staying within the code."

Jim's eyes flew over to the panel, then back to Vic. "Oh, I wondered what that was. Well, then, go ahead." He opened the door and gestured for Vic to enter the room.

Vic started toward the door, then stopped short. "Now, look here. There may be an issue." He gestured for the guards to join him at the door and they fell for it, entering the room behind Vic. Carlotta and Kate slipped into the room just after them.

"What is it?" Jim asked.

"See this crack here?" Vic pointed to the side of the door. "There's a little rusting. I'm not sure if it meets code." He pulled out a tape measure and started measuring.

Jim frowned at the door. "Where's the knob?"

"Doesn't have one," Vic answered. "It opens only from the steam tunnel side. That's why we have to watch the rust accumulation. We can't have people getting into those tunnels from the museum. It's dangerous in there. But the rust here is below the spec so you're okay."

The guards watched while Vic took out a small tool and tapped on the door in various places. He paused after each tap, looked thoughtful and then wrote something on the clipboard. To anyone watching, it all seemed very official, but Kate knew he was buying time and trying to distract the guards so she could get the painting.

Meanwhile, Kate plugged in her vacuum cleaner. She didn't know how she was going to get the money out that Max insisted they leave, but she wanted to make it look like she was actually getting ready to clean. Gideon had rigged the vacuum so that it would actually work, but he'd also done a few modifications to it. Kate hoped she wouldn't hit the wrong switch by mistake. On the other side of the room, Carlotta took out a feather duster and started to dust.

As Vic went about his inspection, Kate moved slowly over to the table with the painting. It was only an eight-inch by ten-inch and she had a special pouch in her uniform made specifically for hiding it.

The best case scenario was that she'd be able to un-obtrusively slip the painting into the pouch, then she and Carlotta could simply walk out as cleaning ladies, leaving the special vacuum with the money behind. You couldn't count on best case scenarios, though, so they had a 'plan b' which involved a hasty exit out through the steam tunnels.

It was now or never. Kate reached out toward the painting slowly.

"Hey! Stop right there!" Jim's agitated voice yelled from the other side of the room. He pressed a red button on the wall and a door flew open. A familiar man ran in, assessed the situation and darted for Kate, who was clutching the edge of the painting in one hand.

In two quick strides, he was on the opposite side of the table, the gold serpent ring gleaming as he grabbed the other side of the painting.

Vic karate chopped Brian, who fell to the floor in a heap.

Jim pulled his gun, but apparently he couldn't decide who to point it at. He stood there, wavering it back and forth between Vic, Carlotta and Kate.

"Hand it over!" Snake Ring tugged on the painting, but Kate had a firm hold on her side.

She tugged back.

Out of the corner of her eye, she could see Carlotta backing toward the steam tunnel door. Vic gave the triple tap on the door that was their signal.

Where was Gertie?

Snake Ring pulled on the painting again and Kate stumbled forward into the edge of the table, but she didn't let go. She dug in her heels and braced against the sturdy table, then yanked back.

The sounds of an alarm vaguely registered in the back of her mind—she was totally focused on getting that painting away from Snake Ring. He put both his hands on the painting and pulled hard, but Kate was ready—she leaned backwards as he tried to wrench it away from her.

Rip!

Kate stumbled back, staring in horror at the half of a painting in her hand.

Across from her, Snake Ring stared at the other half he held in his hand with much the same expression on his face.

Clatter.

The wooden stretchers that the canvas had been stretched across had splintered in the tug-of war and something had fallen out of a hollowed-out space in the wood. It skittered across the floor, sliding to a stop in front of Kate. She barely registered what it was—a small figure of some sort—before swooping it up as quickly as possible.

As she did so, a door on the other side of the room flew open and three masked men came in, waving guns.

"Put it down! Hands in the air!"

Jim and Snake Ring whirled around. Snake Ring pulled a gun with the hand that wasn't holding the painting and pointed it at the three men.

Who were these guys? Were they not with the museum? Why would Jim and Snake Ring point guns at them?

Kate's heart pounded as she clutched her half of the painting to her chest.

What was going on here?

She eyed the other half of the painting, but Snake Ring was still gripping it.

Over at the steam door, Vic and Carlotta had pulled out guns. Kate knew they would only use them as a last resort.

Why hadn't Gertie opened the door from the other side yet?

With everyone pointing guns at each other, it was like a Mexican standoff and Kate knew they needed to create a distraction to make a getaway. She glanced behind her at the plug then down at the vacuum cleaner, wishing she'd paid more attention when Gideon had described what all the various switches and buttons were for. She flipped open one end of the vacuum cleaner, pressed the red button and said a silent prayer that she'd done the right thing.

A few heart-stopping seconds of nothing, then the vacuum whirred. Everyone turned toward the noise. Kate felt a puff of warm air come out of the machine and then an explosion of money burst out, whirling into the air like a green tornado.

The room was covered in a blizzard of hundred dollar bills. They swirled in the air, catching everyone's attention. Guns clattered to the floor as everyone freed up their hands to grab at the airborne money.

"Come on!" Vic yelled.

The steam tunnel door cracked open revealing a dank, black tunnel. Carlotta dove in and Kate made a run for it, reaching the door in record time. Vic barreled through behind her.

Kate turned and looked back into the room. Her eyes collided with those of one of the masked men. Her heart jerked in her chest.

She recognized those eyes—they belonged to FBI agent, and her former partner, Ace Mason. She strained for a closer look just as Gertie slammed the door shut and turned the locking wheel, sealing the door and preventing anyone on the other side from coming after them.

CHAPTER SEVEN

W hy would the FBI be in the museum with masks on?" Gertie asked as they made their way down the steam tunnel.

"Good question." Kate switched on her hardhat light. The LED lights everyone had affixed to the front of their hats illuminated the tunnel pretty well, though Kate wasn't sure if she wanted to see what was in the tunnel, judging from the slimy, moldy sides. She stepped gingerly over the piles of decayed leaves and thought about Ace Mason.

Ace had been her partner at the FBI. More than a partner, actually, but she didn't want to think about that part. They had been assigned to take down one of the most evil adversaries of the FBI—Damian Darkstone.

They'd worked together closely for months on the case. Very closely. Too closely. In the end, they'd gotten their man, but Kate had had to use some unorthodox methods.

She figured that was a minor detail. Everyone knew the world was better off with Darkstone behind bars. Too bad Ace Mason was one of those guys that liked to go 'by the book'. In the end, his testimony had gotten her fired from the FBI, ending their partnership and whatever else they had going.

But that was all ancient history now. Whatever Ace was doing in the museum was no concern of Kate's, unless it had something to do with the painting.

"Are you sure he didn't recognize you?" Gertie was asking.

Kate looked down at her cleaning lady get-up. "I don't think so, I don't look like myself and I even have colored contacts. There's no way he could have known it was me."

"Maybe it wasn't him, Kitten," Vic said. "He had a mask on, so all you saw were eyes."

Kate felt a little put out because it sounded like her father might be defending Ace, which was funny because Vic had never liked him until the previous summer, when he'd had to team up with Ace to rescue Kate and Carlotta. Somehow, the two of them had formed a bond. Ace had tried to make up with Kate then, too, but she wasn't ready for it and she sure didn't need her father sticking up for the guy.

"Yeah, it probably wasn't him," Sylvia piped in. "What would the FBI be doing knocking off a museum?"

"Maybe Ace is moonlighting?" Gertie suggested.

Kate almost laughed, but then a rustling sound up

ahead caught her attention. Her blood turned to ice.

"What's that?" She hated the shaky edge to her voice. "Are there snakes in here?"

Gertie shrugged. "Might be. Everything else is down here. I saw a big fat rat earlier."

Something scurried over Kate's foot and she froze. A tiny squeak escaped from her mouth.

Carlotta turned back to look at her, a frown creasing her forehead. She knew about Kate's snake phobia, but hadn't seen her daughter actually freeze up since she was ten years old. "What is it?"

Kate couldn't say anything. She just stood there with the deer in the headlights look and her heart in her throat. She felt weak, her vision blurry. There wasn't much that stopped her in her tracks, but snakes freaked her out. She felt the same sinking feeling she'd felt in Stockholm. It was as if she were sinking into a black abyss, helpless to move her limbs or speak.

"Kate!" Carlotta was shaking her shoulder and Kate managed to slide her eyes over to look at her mother.

Carlotta tapped her cheek lightly. "Kate, snap out of it. There're no snakes here. That was a cute little mouse."

Carlotta's voice broke through the haze in Kate's brain. Right, it was just a mouse.

"And anyway," Carlotta continued. "You can handle a little thing like a snake. You've handled much worse."

Like Damian Darkstone, Kate thought.

Carlotta's soothing words brought Kate back from the edge. "Take a deep breath," Carlotta commanded.

Kate did as she was told. She sucked in a deep breath, her chest expanding as far as it could. She held the breath until she started to feel dizzy.

"Now let it out."

Kate whooshed out the breath and started to feel normal again. Then she started to feel ridiculous. Who froze like that over a stupid reptile? She was tougher than that.

"What are you guys doing?" Vic's voice echoed from further down the tunnel. "We need to get a move on here. We don't know if they will send someone down one of the other tunnels and cut off our exit."

"They can't," Gertie said. "The only entrances between here and our exit are blocked up, so it's smooth sailing for us."

"Where is the exit?" Carlotta asked.

"Alleyway on Smith Street. Just jimmy open the manhole cover and climb out. Sal is waiting in a car for us."

"What would they send someone in for, anyway?" Kate looked down at the ripped painting with a sinking stomach. "I ruined the painting. This was all for nothing."

"Not nothing. You got half of it." Gertie gestured to the painting and Kate held it up to assess the damage.

"Yeah, sure, but what good is it now?" Kate asked.

Sylvia looked over Gertie's shoulder at the painting. "Wait a minute. Let me see that."

Sylvia leaned forward, angling her head to see the painting better. Kate heard her sharp intake of breath.

"Yeah, I know. It's trash now," Kate said. "Max is going to be really mad. And I left the money so he's out all that money and I only got half a painting. Even if we had the other half, it's not going to be worth much now that it's ripped."

"I wouldn't be too sure about that." Sylvia's voice was tinged with excitement. "If I'm not mistaken, this painting is the *Secret of Itizuma*. The painting disappeared fifty years ago. Very few people have ever seen it and there were no pictures of it, so I can't be certain ... but from what I've heard, this looks like it could fit the bill."

"Great. I ruined a valuable, famous work of art."

"Well, it's not so much the painting itself that was so valuable. The painting reputedly has clues that could help archaeologists solve a five hundred year old mystery."

"What's that?" Carlotta asked.

"The location of the tomb of Itizuma."

CHAPTER EIGHT

I didn't say anything to either of you about my suspicions because I wasn't sure the painting Estelle had really was the *Secret of Itizuma*," Max said through Gideon's speakerphone two days later as they were sitting in the lab at the *Ritzholdt Museum*. "This whole legend is a well-guarded secret that only a few people know about. I couldn't be positive until we got it in-house."

"I didn't know a thing about it myself, but I've done a bit of research and I think it's the real deal." Gideon frowned at the half-painting that lay stretched out on one of his tables next to a folder stuffed with research. "Of course, I only have half of it to look at."

Kate grimaced and Gideon hastened to add. "But it was actually a blessing in disguise that the painting ripped in half because otherwise we would have never discovered the icon hidden inside the wooden stretchers." Gideon pointed to the little figure that had fallen out of the painting when it ripped in half.

Max laughed. "All these years, everyone thought the clues were in the actual painting when maybe they were really hidden inside a hollowed out compartment *in* the stretchers."

"And we never would've discovered that if Kate hadn't gotten into a tug-of-war with it," Gideon smiled.

Kate simply sat in her chair and beamed. She'd expected Max to be mad that the painting had been ripped in half, but apparently it turned out she was a hero. Too bad she couldn't see the expression on Max's face because he was out of town and Gideon could only raise him on speakerphone. Gideon had emailed Max pictures of the painting and the little gold figure. Kate glanced over at it and repressed a shudder—it was a snake in the shape of a figure eight, swallowing its own tail. Yech.

"So that's what Markovic wanted with it, then? He must have gotten the same lead you did and planned to decipher the painting so he could follow the clues to this Aztec burial tomb," Kate asked.

"Yes. The painting disappeared over fifty years ago, but I'd gotten a lead that a famous archaeologist, Reginald White, had it in his possession. He passed away some years ago but the painting never resurfaced. Of course, it was all based on rumors and, since no one alive had ever actually seen the painting and there were no pictures of it, that made tracking it down difficult.

"I figured it was worth the investment because finding that tomb would be a huge coup for the museum. The only other Aztec tomb that has been found is that of

Emperor Ahuizotl which was found under modern-day Mexico City, but that tomb is submerged in water."

"Sounds like something like that would be very valuable," Kate said.

"We could be discovering untold riches, not to mention the historical significance," Gideon added.

"That's right," Max said. "Reginald White researched the Aztecs extensively and had some archaeological finds in Mexico. But when I contacted his family, they didn't have the painting. Much of his collection had been sold off in an auction by Sotheby's, but their records showed no such painting either. We knew the painting would be a landscape of a desert area with hills and nothing they sold matched the description.

"And then one of the family members told me about the big estate sale and I was able to track down the person who ran it and get a listing of what was sold. On that listing were several paintings. I tracked down each one and this was the only one that fit the bill, so I sent Kate out to acquire it and the rest is history."

Gideon twisted his mouth as he looked at the painting. "I think the painting itself might still hold clues but the figure is most important. I've dated it to fourteen twenty-five"

"That's about the right timeframe for Itizuma," Max said. "But what we don't know is how it got in the stretcher. Clearly the painting is of a much later date—it's only about three hundred years old."

"I inspected the stretchers and it looks like the painting was re-stretched at some point," Gideon said.

"So someone somewhere in the last three hundred

years wanted to leave some clues to this guy's tomb," Kate said.

Gideon nodded. "Also, I can see where someone has been trying to use solvents to see if there is an under-painting. That looks recent and I suspect that's what they were doing at the *Lowenstaff* under the guise of restoration."

"I'm not surprised they would think the clue would be an under-painting. That's what I thought, too, and it wouldn't be the first time something was painted over something else that was much more important," Max said.

"But in this case, the clues go deeper." Gideon tapped the figure. "This figure is symbolic. I've traced its origins to an area in Mexico just outside the Mayan ruins of Tulum."

"The Aztecs were mostly situated in Mexico City, but Itizuma was an early ruler and I have heard he was near the coast," Max said.

"That's right. And it's also where Reginald White did some serious archaeology back in the day."

"Well, it looks like we have a lot to go on to try to find this tomb," Kate said.

"We have a lot, but we don't have everything," Gideon cautioned. "Markovic still has the other half of the painting and possibly other clues that might've been inside the stretcher."

"Sure, but this seems like enough to go on. The figure is certainly a clue, although I don't know what the painting means. But if we take a little trip out there, maybe it will become evident," Kate said. A trip to Mexico was looking mighty appealing, especially since she didn't want to go back to her desk and shuffle more papers.

"I agree with Kate," Max said.

"There is one other problem," Gideon added.

"What's that?"

"Kate swears one of the masked men inside the *Lowenstaff* was Ace Mason." Gideon glanced at Kate for confirmation and she nodded.

"What would the FBI be doing in disguise and why would they be interested in this painting?" Max asked.

"That's what I was wondering," Gideon answered.

"Well, you know the government. They have to get their hands into everything," Max said. "Sounds like they might've been on some sort of an undercover mission, or maybe it wasn't the FBI. Kate could have been mistaken. I mean, they did have masks on, right?

"Right." Kate's top teeth worried her bottom lip. The men had been wearing masks, but she was sure the person she'd locked eyes with was Ace. On the other hand, it did seem crazy to think that the FBI would be breaking into the museum like that. Everyone else was probably right she must've just *thought* it was Ace.

"I just think we might need extra caution on this. Markovic's people might be following clues along the same trail and who knows what these other people are doing. Whether they are the FBI or not, we have to watch out for them," Gideon said.

"I trust you'll outfit Kate with the appropriate tools for the job and we'll put surveillance on Markovic's people so we know their every move," Max said.

"I'm sure I can handle it," Kate said. She wasn't afraid

of Onion Mole, Snake Ring or Ace Mason. She could take care of herself and she was intrigued by this find. Being the first to uncover an Aztec emperor's burial tomb would be a huge coup for the museum and a heck of a lot of fun.

"Okay, well that leaves only one problem, then," Gideon said.

Kate's brows tugged together. "What?"

Gideon opened the folder that lay next to the painting and leafed through a few of the pages. "According to my research, the *secret of Itizuma* comes with a curse."

"A curse?" Kate scoffed. "Don't tell me you believe in some stupid old curse?"

"Well, I think Reginald White should have believed in it. You know that he disappeared mysteriously on an expedition to find the tomb, right?"

Kate's laugh was a bit higher-pitched than usual. "I doubt that had anything to do with a curse. I'm sure there's a logical explanation. The tomb is in a remote place, right? He could have been attacked by animals or something. What, exactly, is this curse, anyway?"

Gideon adjusted his coke bottle glasses, picked up the page and held it close to his face. "According to what it says here, the curse says something like this—'He who takes of greed will suffer with need in time.'"

"What's that supposed to mean?" Kate asked. "It doesn't even really rhyme."

"I don't know what it means, but do you want to suffer with need? I know I sure don't."

"Hold on there," Max cut in. "I know all about this curse and apparently so does Markovic. That's why I sent you out to the museum with money. So that we wouldn't be 'taking'. We paid for that painting fair and square, so we shouldn't suffer the curse. Not that I believe in curses, but it's better to be safe than sorry."

"That sounds good to me," Kate said.

Gideon shrugged. "Well, if you guys aren't worried then I'm not. I did some additional research and came up with the name of a guy you can talk to about the tomb. I can arrange a meeting. Not sure how accurate what he has to say will be, but it's better than nothing."

"I can be on a plane tomorrow." Kate batted away the doubts that flapped around in her brain like rabid bats. She didn't believe in curses.

Her glance fell on the ripped canvas that lay on the table. She was sure that the fact that they would probably *need* the other half of the painting to find the tomb was just a minor bump in their plan and had nothing to do with a stupid curse.

CHAPTER NINE

The open-air market was alive with activity. Kate looked around at the blankets, clothing, fruits and vegetables. She contemplated buying one of the large, colorful shopping bags and stuffing it with produce to bring back to her hotel.

The thought of her hotel brought a sigh to her lips. It was decent, not top-notch, but Kate didn't really need a top notch hotel. That wasn't what made her sigh, though. It was the company.

Max hadn't wanted her alone on the job and Gideon had spilled the beans to her parents, who just 'happened' to have always wanted to go to Mexico on vacation. They agreed to eagerly combine that with helping out Kate. If Kate found the site, Max would get the appropriate permits and send a crew out to dig, but for now, it was just her and her folks.

Kate had to admit she was a little put out and she couldn't help but wonder if her parents' eagerness to accompany her had anything to do with her freezing up in the steam tunnel. It would be just like her mother to spill the beans to Gideon and he would probably tell Max. Maybe they were all worried she would freeze up again.

She knew they had the best of intentions, but she could do her job without her parents watching over her and she hardly thought that fumbling around in the jungle for an old tomb would require the skills of a jewel thief and a con artist. Then again, one never knew. At least the weather was warm and the area was gorgeous, with the high bluffs overlooking a white sand beach and aqua ocean.

Thoughts of the beach evaporated as she scanned the market, looking for her contact. Gideon had set up a meeting with a local man who had information—handed down from his family—on the location of the tomb.

She strolled the aisles, taking in the smell of roasting meat, the sound of children playing, the cluck of chickens. She passed colorful stalls loaded with lush fruit and vegetables.

She walked at a slow pace, looking for a small hut with an indigo print curtain. Gideon and told her a man would be inside the hut and would be expecting her. Her eyes raked the crowd, her heart skittering when she spotted the curtain. Just inside, an old man, his face a map of wrinkles, sat on a stool. In front of him, smoke drifted out of a hookah. Behind him, the inside of the hut was pitch black.

Kate hesitated just outside the hut watching the man,

trying to guess his age. He looked ancient. His skin was dark and incredibly wrinkled, his black hair shot with gray. He looked up, piercing her with brilliant blue eyes. He gave an imperceptible nod.

"Matzaleah?" Kate gave the code word Gideon had told her to use.

The man nodded and gestured for her to enter. She stepped inside and, with one swift motion, the man shut the curtain, cutting off the sunlight that had been warming her shoulders, surrounding her in darkness.

Kate felt a niggle of doubt take root in her stomach. Maybe it wasn't such a great idea to come here alone.

The pungent, spicy smoke filled the hut. Kate focused on breathing through her nose, hoping to filter out the effects of whatever it was the guy had going in his pipe.

The sound of water bubbled out of the pipe as the man took a toke through a flexible hose whose resemblance to a snake made Kate shudder. He turned his brilliant blue eyes on her.

"So, you want to know about the legend," he said.

Kate nodded.

Light filtered in around the curtains in the front and back and between the cracks in the flimsy walls of the hut which was empty except for the man, his obnoxious pipe and a plain, wooden stool. The man gestured for Kate to sit on the stool and she did. She started to relax—maybe because the man seemed harmless, or maybe it was the effects of the secondhand smoke. She wasn't sure which. She pulled the stool up and took a seat.

The man held his palm up toward her. Kate remembered that Gideon had told her the man would expect payment. Silver coins. She dug them out of her pocket and dropped them into his palm.

He looked at them, flipping each one over, and then smiled a toothless smile as he slipped them into his own pocket. He leaned forward, his elbows resting on his knees.

"The legend is old, from my great-great-great-grandfather's time," he said. "Many think this is the area of the Mayans, but the Aztecs that came after them were great rulers here, too. My grandfather was descended from these rulers and the old stories were passed down through the generations."

Kate nodded. She wasn't sure what to say. She didn't really care about the guy's grandfather or his legends. She just wished the guy would get on with it and tell her where the tomb was.

"Many have tried to find the burial place of Itizuma." The man's face darkened. "And many have failed."

"Well, hopefully I'll have more success than they did," Kate said.

The man laughed, but it wasn't a pleasant sound. It was ominous, and Kate felt a chill dance up her spine. "You would do well to stay away from the tomb. No good can come of it. Some things should stay buried forever."

Kate straightened on the primitive stool. "That may be the case but there could be significant historical finds in that tomb. Finds that could help us understand the way the Aztecs lived. Wouldn't you want us to find out more about your ancestors?" Kate asked

The man snorted and took another long toke on his hookah. "Is that what you think is there?"

Kate's brow creased. "What else would be there?"

"Perhaps you don't know or perhaps I don't know. I just know of the legends. None of my people will go near there. But you haven't paid me to tell you the dangers of what is inside, you've paid me to tell you *where* the legend says the tomb is and I will comply because to do anything else would be wrong."

"Okay." Kate pushed away the uneasy feeling that was spreading in her chest. The man was probably referring to the curse and they'd taken care of that ... not that she believed in it in the first place.

The hookah bubbled as he took another long toke. He sucked in the smoke, held it and then blew it out in a slow stream that wafted up to the ceiling. Kate's nerves crawled around annoyingly inside her skin as she waited for him to speak.

"The site is outside the town. Fifty miles due north. Take a left when you see the mountain on the old dirt road. It is overgrown there now, almost jungle, but if you look with care, you will see the signs. It is reputed the tomb is near there." The man gave a little half-nod, then pushed the curtain aside, latching it on the corner and letting the light in before turning his attention back to the hookah.

"Thanks." Kate stood. The man nodded slightly and Kate stepped out of the hut.

As the sunlight washed over her, she felt relief, then the familiar excitement started to bubble up inside her. There was nothing Kate loved more than being on the hunt. She sensed that she was just about to discover something extraordinary. She hurried back to the hotel feeling alive with the excitement of the discovery in front of her and the man's ominous words about some things being better left buried quickly forgotten.

CHAPTER TEN

T ake a left at the mountain?" Vic stared at Kate
incredulously after she relayed the details of the
meeting with the hookah man. "What kind of
directions are those?"

Kate shrugged. "That's what he said. I figured we
could use the painting to orient ourselves and figure out
where to take the left."

Vic glanced down at the photocopy of the painting
they'd brought with them. The real painting was still
back at the museum with Gideon who was working on
it to try to see if it would give up any more clues. "Too
bad we only have half of the painting."

"I'm sure we can figure it out," Carlotta yelled from
the bedroom of their suite.

"Anyway," Vic said. "I take it we'll be camping out?"

"I guess so. The man said it was fifty miles from here.

It's not practical to drive there every day and there are no hotels out there. We need to be on site so we can cover ground as quickly as possible. Gideon sent out the appropriate equipment right?"

"Yep." Vic spread his arms to indicate several duffel bags of khaki-colored canvas. "We've got tents, we've got mosquito netting, we've got metal detectors, we've got tools for digging, and we've got weapons."

"Weapons?" Kate's brows tugged. "What do we need those for?"

Vic shrugged. "You never know when you might run into in animal … or an enemy." He picked up a long, javelin-like object and handed it to Kate. "Gideon sent this especially for you. You can swoosh it in the thick underbrush and scare any snakes away. Some of them are poisonous down here, not to mention the other creepy crawlies we don't want to step on."

Kate shuddered at the thought as she took the weapon from her father. It reminded her of a fencing foil or saber with a long, thin blade and a guarded handle at the end. She swished it in the air, thrusting and jabbing as if she were fencing an invisible opponent.

"That reminds me, you were pretty good at fencing in college, weren't you?" Carlotta appeared, leaning against the door frame to the bedroom.

Kate laughed. "Yes, and it looks like I've still got what it takes." She swished the letter 'Z' in the air with a flourish.

"That has a dual purpose. The end of it has a razor-sharp knife," Vic said. "Just press on the side of the handle."

Kate did as told and a gleaming, silver dagger shot out of the end like a switchblade. "I guess I'd better be careful with that." Kate pressed the other side of the handle and the blade retracted.

"Do we need any other supplies? Food?" Kate asked.

"I already stocked up on groceries and packed them in the cooler." Carlotta pointed to a big, red cooler sitting by the door.

Maybe having the folks around wasn't such a bad thing after all, Kate thought. They certainly were thorough and she liked how they had taken care of the details. All she had to do was hop in the car and go.

"I'll just catch up with Gideon and then we can pack the car and leave." Kate looked around the room, spotted the laptop on the table and grabbed it. She flipped open the screen, then logged into Skype and connect with Gideon.

"Hi, Kate. How goes it?" Gideon's smiling face filled the screen.

"Great. How are things back at the shop?"

"Same old, same old. So give me an update. Did you talk to the contact I gave you?" Gideon asked.

Kate told him about her visit with the hookah man and that they were packing up the car now and heading out to the area. "Have you been able to find out any more about the other half of the painting?"

"No. We have a tail on some of Markovic's men, though. We weren't able to get a picture of the other half."

Kate cringed. Why hadn't she thought to take a picture of the painting when she'd been in the museum?

Of course, she never expected that she'd leave with only half of it.

"I've been working on the half you brought back," Gideon continued. "And it does seem like there might be something under the painting. I'm not sure what it is, though. It's very delicate work and I have to go slowly so as not to damage it."

"Of course," Kate said. "In the meantime we'll just work with what we've got."

Gideon nodded. "I sent you out some special gear."

"I got the snake beater," Kate said. "Thanks. Looks like that could come in handy."

"There's something else. In the striped duffel bag, you will find a funky-looking watch. That's going to be our communication device out at the site. There's no cell phone tower out there, you know."

Kate hadn't thought about that. She found the striped duffel bag and rummaged inside, pulling out a watch with a white band and a large face.

"This one?" She held the watch up to her laptop camera so Gideon could see.

"Yes, that's the one. I've rigged it so that we can communicate via one of the satellites."

"I didn't know you could access satellites."

Gideon leaned closer to his computer and lowered his voice. "Technically, I'm not supposed to. I kind of hacked in to one of the government satellites, so don't tell anyone. Especially the FBI. Anyway, the satellite is in an oval orbit and we'll only be able to communicate when it is overhead, a different time each day. Tomorrow, that time is twelve fifteen."

"Okay." Kate fiddled with the watch that showed a digital display of the time. She pressed a button and got a screen filled with static. Another button told her the weather.

"We'll only have a fifteen-minute window, so make sure you have all your information on hand and ready. Make your reports brief and concise. Compile a list of things you need me to send ahead of time."

"Will do." Kate strapped the watch onto her wrist.

"Anything else?" Gideon asked.

"Nope. I'll check back in with you tomorrow at twelve fifteen."

"Okay. Over and out. Oh, and Kate?"

The edge in Gideon's voice tore her attention from the watch and she looked at her laptop screen to see his concerned, green eyes looking back. "Yes?"

"Be careful. Markovic's people have the other half of the painting and they're bound to find out you're in Mexico. Keep your eyes peeled for them."

Kate's heart flooded with warmth at her friend's concern. "Don't worry. I will."

"Okay, then. Over and out." Gideon's face disappeared and the screen went dark.

Kate logged out of Skype, shut down the laptop and packed it in the bag which she brought out to the Jeep where Vic and Carlotta were waiting. They'd packed the whole thing while she'd been on Skype with Gideon and were sitting in the front. Kate climbed into the back.

"This will be just like one of our old camping trips we took when you were a kid," Vic said.

"I don't know about that, Dad. I think this one could

be a little more dangerous."

"Danger is my middle name." Vic shoved his dark sunglasses up onto his forehead and twisted in his seat to look at her, his blue eyes dark with concern. "That's never concerned you before. Don't tell me you're having second thoughts about this."

Kate straightened in her seat. She wasn't having second thoughts and she certainly wasn't going to freeze up, if that's what they thought—curse or no curse. "Not at all. Full speed ahead."

Vic slid the sunglasses back down over his eyes, turned forward and drove north.

CHAPTER ELEVEN

They'd been driving for forty-five minutes when Kate saw the plume of dust behind them. Someone was following them. She twisted in her seat to get a better look.

"Do you see that?"

"What?" Carlotta angled the side mirror.

"I think someone is following us." Kate squinted but the dust was gone. The road had turned from dirt to thick underbrush and was getting narrower the further they drove.

Kate glanced back again, but the dust plume was gone. Maybe it had been her imagination.

"We're coming up on the fifty-mile mark. How accurate do you think this guy's story was?" Vic asked.

Kate scanned the horizon, comparing it to the picture of the painting she had in her lap. Was the painting of the same place? It was hard to tell. The painting had been done long ago and perhaps vegetation had grown up since then.

She did see a big hill in the distance, similar to the one in the painting. In the painting, though, there were huts and structures that looked almost like a little primitive village. She didn't see any of that here.

"I see a hill that looks like it could be the one in the painting and the man said take a left near the hill."

"There's a left coming up." Carlotta pointed to a dirt road. "Should we take it?"

"Your guess is as good as mine. I guess we need to start somewhere so we might as well try it. Besides, it's getting late and we should set up camp."

Vic took the left and they traveled about another mile before they saw some interesting-looking rocks. Rocks that didn't actually look like regular rocks. Kate remembered the man saying something about seeing the signs. "Let's stop here. I want to look at these rocks."

They stopped and examined the rocks.

"Do you think these could be sacrificial stones?" Carlotta shuddered as she bent down to get a closer look at one.

"I don't know. The way they are worn doesn't look quite natural." The granite rocks were fairly smooth on the top—not polished, but flat naturally. The divots in them seemed smoother than they would normally be, as if some force had worked on them over and over again. They were covered with moss.

"In any case, this makes a pretty good place to set up camp," Vic said.

They spent the next two hours setting up their tents, along with a lean-to and some tarps. Gideon had thought of everything and they even had a folding picnic table that Carlotta set up next to the fire pit Vic had made by arranging large stones in a circle.

Once they were done, Carlotta pulled out the cooler, opened it and sat on one of the large rocks while she rummaged through. "It's getting close to dinner time. What do you guys say we make supper and come up with a plan of action while we eat?"

"Good idea." Kate pulled over the duffel bag that had paper plates, cups and napkins while Vic started the fire.

Twenty minutes later, Carlotta had set a metal grate over the coals and put a cast iron pan on top of the crackling fire. The smell of charred hot-dogs made Kate's mouth water.

The cooler had been placed on the other side of the camp, far from the fire, and Kate went over to dig out ketchup. As she bent over, rifling through the contents, a rustling sound in the jungle behind the cooler caught her attention. She looked around nervously for her snake stick.

"Are there snakes out here?" she asked.

"Probably, but I don't think they'll bother us near the fire," Carlotta answered.

"I hear something out there." Kate cocked her head. She did hear rustling, didn't she? That seemed like a lot of rustling for a snake.

Carlotta and Vic exchanged a glance. "I don't hear anything," Carlotta said.

Were her parents going deaf? She could hear it, clear

as day. They *were* getting older. Maybe they just couldn't hear as well anymore.

"I distinctly hear rustling." Kate lowered her voice and crept back to toward the tent where she'd seen Vic put the weapons. "Someone is out there."

Kate's heartbeat picked up speed as she cast around for the weapons bag.

"Kate there's nothing out there," Vic said.

Maybe her parents had been retired too long and their senses weren't honed to look for danger like she was.

"Come on and sit down." Carlotta patted the rock beside her.

Kate glanced at the rock, then back at the bushes. It was almost dark but she could see the dense foliage moving. That was no snake out there. It was something big and it was headed right for them.

Kate lunged for her snake stick that was leaning against a tree on the other side of the camp. She pressed the button and the dagger slid out, then she tensed her legs and got ready.

"Do I smell hot dogs?" Gertie burst out of the undergrowth with Benny, Sal and Frankie following close behind.

"What the heck? What are you guys doing in the jungle?" Kate asked, still pointing the business end of her snake stick at them.

"Hey, watch that." Frankie nodded toward the stick and Kate relaxed.

"Sorry, dear, we invited them." Carlotta grimaced. "We thought it would be a nice surprise."

"And safer with more people," Vic added.

"Why didn't you guys just come down the road?" Kate pointed to the dirt road.

"We were exploring," Benny said. "Our four-wheelers are about a half-mile that away." He pointed back in the direction they'd come from.

"You're going to need some people to help dig out this tomb." Benny punctuated the words by stabbing the front of the metal shovel he was carrying into the ground and leaning on the handle.

"Max is going to send out a crew if we find the tomb," Kate pointed out.

"Oh, well." Sal reached toward the hot dogs. He clicked his prosthetic thumb and a corkscrew slid out, which he then used to skewer a hot dog. "It'll be fun looking for the tomb even if we don't dig it out. I'm sure you can use extra people to help look, right?" Sal raised his brows at Kate as he nibbled the end of the hot dog.

"Sure." She could use all the help she could get. And her father did have a point. It would be safer with more people out here in the middle of nowhere.

"So, that was you guys behind us?" Kate asked.

"Reckon so. We'll just grab some food and then get our machines and set up right here. We can take shifts watching the camp. It's getting dark and we don't know what's out here." Gertie gestured toward the area outside the camp which looked much scarier to Kate now that it was dark and she couldn't see more than two feet beyond their camp.

Gertie, Sal, Bennie and Frankie ate a few bites, then scurried off in the direction they'd come from, turning on their large LED head lamps. About twenty minutes later, Kate heard the sound of engines, and they pulled up to camp in four-wheelers, slinging their gear off the machines and setting up small tents while Carlotta broke out some graham crackers, marshmallows and chocolate bars.

The seven of them sat around a campfire and Kate felt like she was a kid at summer camp licking gooey toasted marshmallow off her fingers as the others entertained each other with ghost stories.

They came up with a schedule of shifts so someone would always be on watch. Not that it was necessary, but Vic said one could never be too safe and Kate agreed.

They'd also come up with a plan to scour the area the next day for signs of the tomb.

Kate fell asleep sometime around midnight, feeling safe and secure with her extended family watching over her. She was so content that she almost forgot she was out there in search of the tomb of a long-dead Aztec emperor … a discovery that might come with a deadly curse.

CHAPTER TWELVE

The next morning, they split up into teams and spread out in different directions, figuring they could cover more area that way. Kate went east with Sal and Carlotta, all three of them armed with multi-pocketed vests that contained the essentials—compasses, water, bug spray, machetes, stun guns and a GPS tracker to mark reference points.

"This undergrowth is thick." Sal whacked away at a leathery frond, the serrated edge of which was as sharp as a knife. "And dangerous." He held up his prosthetic thumb, which had a slice in it from the leaf to prove his point.

"I'll say." Kate stayed directly behind him, swishing her walking stick back and forth to ward off any snakes that might be coiled at the sides of the path.

"All the better for the bugs to hide in," Carlotta added as she swatted away the zillionth mosquito of the day.

Kate heard something to the left and froze. "What's that?"

"What?" Carlotta froze behind her.

Sal had stopped in front of her. "I didn't hear anything. It's probably a monkey."

Kate turned in a slow circle. He was right. She was being paranoid. Who else would be out here besides them and some monkeys? Markovic's people couldn't have followed her here this soon unless his half of the painting yielded the same clues as hers.

She took one nervous glance around, then followed Sal forward. "We'd better stop soon. I have to contact Gideon at twelve fifteen."

"No problem," Sal said. "I could use a rest. I think I see a less dense area up ahead with some rocks. Maybe we can set down there."

They forged ahead slowly. Kate kept her eyes on the ground, wondering how they would ever notice any signs of a civilization from centuries ago in this thick vegetation.

They came into an area where they could at least walk without having to clear a path. Sal hefted himself onto a large rock and took out his canteen. Carlotta did the same, untying the bandanna from her neck and soaking it with water. Kate laid down on top of a large rock and looked up at small pieces of sky that poked through the dense leaves of the tall trees. She was happy for the shade—otherwise, the heat would have been brutal.

At twelve fifteen her watch beeped. "Time to talk to Gideon."

She looked at her wrist, fiddling with the buttons until Gideon's face appeared.

"Kate! How are you?" Gideon asked.

"Fine. We had quite the camp out last night and are perusing the area today looking for signs of ancient civilizations."

"Any luck?"

"Not really. The foliage is very thick here. There could be an ancient Aztec tomb ten feet away and we'd miss it," Kate sighed. "It's going to take a while to go over the area thoroughly unless that painting has given up some more specific clues."

"I'm afraid not. I haven't been able to figure out the meaning of what I found under the painting yet. It could be some sort of a primitive code."

"That would be great."

"In the meantime, I wanted to warn you that word on the street is that Markovic is onto us. He knows you are in Mexico and has dispatched a team there, too."

Kate felt worry bloom in her chest. "Does he know where we are?"

"I'm not sure. I don't know what clues were on his half of the map … and also Ace Mason was here in the office and he made some funny comments about the *Lowenstaff Museum*. I think you were right about him being there and he might have recognized you."

Kate whooshed out a breath. "You don't think he's coming here, too, do you?"

"I doubt it. What would the FBI care about an old Aztec tomb?"

"What would they care about that painting in the museum?"

"Good point." Gideon's voice crackled and the display got snowy for a second.

"Gideon? You there?"

"Yes. The satellite is almost out of range. There's one more thing I wanted to tell you."

"What?"

"There's another archaeologist in the area. Jersey Swan. I actually know her from some work I did for my master's thesis."

Kate frowned "She's here looking for the tomb, too?"

"I don't think so. She filed with the government to research the ruins of a Mayan village in the area. I suspect she has no idea about the Aztec tomb, since this is typically an area where they find Mayan remains. The Aztecs were mostly near Mexico City."

"Right."

"Anyway, Max said it would be good for you to keep the real reason for your trip secret. We alerted the appropriate people that you are also looking for Mayan archaeology so you won't get any trouble from the government."

"Do you think Jersey is going to be a problem?" Kate gnawed her bottom lip.

Gideon shook his head. "I don't think so. But naturally, you don't want to encroach on her territory. On the other hand, it might be a good idea to check out what she's doing. She may have stumbled across something that would be important to our project."

Kate looked around the dense area. "How will I even find her? I mean, you can barely see ten feet into the woods here."

"Hey, that's your job." Gideon's voice broke up into bits of static. " … like … satellite … out of range ... tomorrow twelve thirty …" And the screen went blank.

"Well, sounds like this jungle is going to get pretty crowded, what with these Markovic people, the FBI and this Jersey girl," Sal said.

"No kidding." Kate slapped at a mosquito that buzzed her ear. She wasn't going to worry about all the company, though. It seemed impossible they would run into each other way out in the middle of nowhere. Not only that, but she'd be lucky if she could find any clues to Itizuma's tomb at all.

Carlotta slid off the rock. "I guess we should continue forward."

Kate grabbed her walking stick and took the lead. Now that the foliage wasn't as dense, they could move faster. Twenty minutes later, they came across an area that gave Kate pause.

"It doesn't look quite natural here." Kate spun around, taking in the placement of the rocks. There were lots of ferns growing up and moss, but it looked almost as if things had been placed strategically.

"Look at this!" Carlotta lifted the leaves of some sort of giant palm shrub to reveal what looked like stone steps. Crudely made, but steps nonetheless.

"It looks like steps," Sal said.

"I think you're right. It's so overgrown, it's hard to tell

what might have been here hundreds of years ago, but there definitely was something." Kate pulled out her GPS and marked the spot. "I'll mark these and we'll add it to the map when we get back to camp. Maybe the others have found something, too, and an overall view of the different areas of interest might give us something more solid to go on."

Carlotta twisted her mouth as she looked around, poking under leaves and glancing off into the distance. "Something's not right about this place. It looks like people have been here and there's a thin path through the trees over there." Carlotta pointed to where the vegetation got dense again. Kate could see a thin path.

The three of them walked toward it.

"Look at this." Sal pointed to a flattened area and the three of them took a step forward for a better look.

"This ground feels awfully spongy …" Carlotta said—exactly what Kate was thinking—and then the ground shifted under Kate's feet. She jerked her head up, looking at Carlotta and Sal whose faces mirrored the alarm she was feeling.

"Oh, no, I think we—" Kate's words were cut off by the sinking sensation of the ground disappearing beneath her feet and the heart-thudding panic of free-falling through thin air.

CHAPTER THIRTEEN

Pain shot through Kate's right side as she landed in a jolting crunch on the damp earth. The wind whooshed out of her lungs. She gasped for breath, trying to sit up, holding her throbbing elbow close into her body.

"What happened?" Sal shook his head and pushed up onto all fours.

"We fell into a pit." Carlotta was already standing, inspecting the side of the six foot square pit.

Kate caught her breath and managed to stand, shaking out her right arm and testing all her limbs. Fingers, toes, knees—everything seemed to be in good working order, if a bit bruised.

Looking up, she saw her mother was right. The pit was about nine feet deep. The roots that protruded from the rough-dug sides reminded Kate of snakes and she shuddered. Panic lapped at her gut as she looked around the inside of the pit to make sure they didn't have company. She looked around for her walking stick and then remembered it had flown out of her hand when she fell. It must still be up top.

"Well, doesn't that beat all. We fell into a trap," Sal said.

"Yeah, but why is there a trap out in the middle of nowhere?" Carlotta asked.

"Not nowhere," Kate pointed out. "We're in the middle of some sort of Mayan ruin."

"And obviously someone doesn't want us exploring any further on that path," Sal said.

"So, something good must be down there," Kate added.

"Do you think it's the same something we're—"
Click!

The unmistakable sound of a shotgun being ratcheted came from above.

Kate looked up, shading her eyes against the sun that glared into the hole from behind two human silhouettes and the long barrel of the shotgun.

Kate's thoughts flew to Onion Mole and Snake Ring. Could they have found her this soon? And how would they have had time to dig a pit? Not to mention that the shotgun was a big departure from their dart gun blunderbus.

"Poachers, just like we thought." The voice wasn't Onion Mole or Snake Ring. It was a woman.

"We're not poachers." Carlotta's hands flew to her hips. "We're here on official business. Just who are *you*?"

"I think we have the advantage, so if you aren't poachers or thieves, you tell us who you are first," the girl said.

"We're with the *Ritzholdt Museum*," Kate said in her most official voice. "Out here on a project."

"And *you* are holding us hostage," Carlotta added in an irate voice.

The woman's shadow bent closer, her long, blonde hair streaming down over the edge of the pit. The other shadow, who Kate could now see was a man with ginger-colored hair and beard, looked over her shoulder.

"Well, I guess they don't look like poachers." The man looked at the woman uncertainly, then called down to them, "Do you have proof?"

Luckily, Kate did have proof. Gideon had packed her official museum ID badge in her safari vest. At the time, she'd laughed at him. Why would she need that in the middle of nowhere? But Gideon usually knew best so she'd kept it in there, and now she was glad she did. She retrieved the leather wallet from her vest and tossed it up toward the woman, who caught it easily.

The woman stared at it, then looked down at Kate and handed it to the man. "They look legit."

The man grunted then lowered the shotgun, passed the wallet back to the woman and disappeared.

"Sorry about that. We're digging out an area just west of here and we've had a big problem with poachers and thieves try to steal some of the artifacts we've been digging up. These pits are our way of discouraging them." She shrugged. "Out here in the jungle, you have to use whatever you can."

"You have an archaeologic dig going on near here?" Kate asked

"Yep."

"Then you must be Jersey Swan. We have a friend in common."

The man returned and tossed a rope ladder over the side, staking the top of it in the ground above. Sal gestured for Kate to go first, and Kate gestured for Carlotta.

"Who's that?" Jersey held her hand out to help Carlotta scale the top of the hole.

"Gideon Crenshaw." Kate started up the ladder.

"Well, why didn't you say so? Any friend of Gid's is a friend of mine." Jersey helped Kate out and the two of them shook hands. "I remember now that he went to work for the *Ritzholdt*. How is he?"

"Just fine. Geeky as ever," Kate said, eliciting a laugh from Jersey. The sound of her laugh was light, a tinkling that matched with her kind, blue eyes and sun-kissed hair and gave her a girl-next-door appeal.

"He always did like science." Jersey put out a hand to help Sal, who waved her off.

"This is Ed, my assistant." Jersey gestured toward the man who was pulling the ladder out of the pit. Kate introduced Carlotta and Sal and they all shook hands and made small talk.

Despite their inauspicious beginning, Kate found herself warming to Jersey, who was actually quite friendly. She even offered them water and a protein bar as they sat around on the steps which, as it turned out, really were from Mayan ruins.

"It's a good thing we weren't stuck in there for any

length of time." Carlotta pointed to the pit. "It could be dangerous."

"Oh, we check them quite regularly," Ed said. "I guess we can have Andy and Tony put the top of the pit back."

"Andy and Tony are our helpers," Jersey explained as she led them back to the area that had the steps. "They're pretty good with certain 'techniques' to discourage theft."

"I think we should note the coordinates of this thing on our GPS," Sal said. "You got any more surprises like this around?"

"We do, but I'll be happy to tell you where they are so you can avoid them." Jersey slid her eyes over to Kate. "So, tell me, what exactly are you out here looking for?"

"We're actually interested in something further north," Kate lied. "I'm on a project that is exploring how the Mayans got fresh water and dealt with the whole issue of plumbing."

"Oh, that's interesting. So you're not really interested in Mayan artifacts?"

"Oh, no, not at all. Our research is purely instructional. We don't want to bring anything back to the museum except knowledge."

"Then what are you doing out here?" Ed asked.

Kate smiled sweetly at him. "Just getting acclimated."

Jersey twisted her lips and regarded Kate. Then, apparently coming to a decision, she said, "It sounds like our goals are complementary. Maybe we can help each other out?"

"That will be great. Unfortunately I don't have much to share right now. We just got here," Kate said

"That's no problem." Jersey stood up, holding her

hand out to help Kate up. "I'll be happy to show you what we've got going and as you find stuff, maybe you could relay that to us."

"Sure, that would be great." Kate glanced at Carlotta and Sal, who both shrugged as if to say 'it's your show, do what you want.' She noticed Ed's scowl, but Jersey seem unfazed as she stepped around the pit and motioned for them to follow her down the path.

They followed her, single file on the thin path, through the dense tropical forest.

"The site back there was just one section of what we think is a larger village," Jersey said as she held back a palm frond so it didn't whip Kate's face. "I think you'll be impressed with what we have at the main site."

Kate focused on swishing her special walking stick, which she'd retrieved from the ground beside the pit, back and forth just in case Jersey's footsteps didn't scare the snakes away.

"I think the entire village encompasses several miles," Jersey continued. "But it's so overgrown here it's almost impossible to see any signs, even if they're right next to you."

"How'd you find the site?" Carlotta asked.

"Research," Jersey said simply.

Carlotta and Kate exchanged a shrug. Apparently, Jersey didn't want to elaborate and Kate couldn't blame her. The archaeology business could be competitive, so one tended to keep one's methods to oneself.

The path ended and they spilled out into a clearing, which was much more interesting than the area where they'd fallen into the pit. It was a larger space with areas where you could clearly see steps, edges of buildings and even the foundation of a rounded building. Off to the right, Kate could see the remnants of a ball court.

"Wow, this is cool." Sal was over at a large stone rectangle carved with Mayan symbols.

"Yes, we think this was the center plaza," Jersey said. "As you can see, though, there aren't any buildings still standing. You can see where they once were, but the rocks are strewn about." Jersey waved her hand around the area.

"It's still a nice find," Kate said.

"Yeah, this is great." Sal pointed to what looked like a stone bench with two large chunks of rock supporting a wide slab on top. "This is a pretty big seat. Did those Mayans have wide butts?"

"Actually, we think it might be a sacrificial stone. You want to try it out?" Jersey joked.

Sal jumped back from the stone and eyed it suspiciously. "No, thanks."

Kate pointed to several tents which were set up in the northwest corner. "Are you camping out right here?"

"Yes. We like to be right in the thick of things. That way, no one can come and steal our artifacts." Jersey walked toward a large, white tent and motioned for them to follow. Inside the tent, long tables were set up. On top of the tables sat an array of objects.

"These are the artifacts we've recovered so far," Jersey said.

Kate walked down the row of tables, which held primitive tools, arrowheads, primitively carved jade beads, bone beads, stingray spines and shells. One of the nicer pieces sat at the very end—the oblong beads of a jade necklace which had been placed in a semicircle in the order where the beads would have been strung together.

"That's a nice piece." Kate pointed to the necklace. "It almost looks like it would be from royalty. Have you found a tomb here?"

"No. We found the pieces when we dug out the remnants of one of the buildings." Jersey lifted the flap of the tent, indicating for them to exit.

"So you haven't found any ruins or evidence of water reservoirs?" Ed had come up to join them.

"Not yet. Today is actually our first day out in the field," Kate said. "We camped out last night to get a head start first thing this morning."

"Where are you camped?" Jersey asked.

"We're a couple miles due east of here," Sal said.

"Is it just the three of you?" Ed asked.

Carlotta narrowed her eyes at him, and Kate figured Carlotta was wondering if Ed was trying to size them up just in case they became adversaries. "No. We have four others in our party."

"Sounds like quite the party," Jersey said.

Sal chuckled, "It *is* like a party."

"Maybe we should get together tonight for supper. We can fill each other in on what we discover today," Jersey said. "We're digging out a promising area and between you and the others on your team, you may have something new."

"That sounds like a good idea." Kate glanced at Carlotta and Sal, who both nodded. She felt a little pang of guilt squeeze her stomach. She had no intention of telling Jersey about anything they found and she certainly wasn't going to reveal the real reason for the mission. But she wanted to keep track of what Jersey was turning up in case it gave her a clue to the tomb she was looking for.

Kate was no expert, but judging by the artifacts on the table this was strictly a Mayan site, so the odds of them uncovering something that would lead to Itizuma's tomb were slim— which made her feel better since she didn't think it was fair to use Jersey's finds for her own gain. That would be almost like stealing and, even though Kate didn't believe in the curse, it was safer to try to avoid doing anything that would invoke it.

Kate pulled out her GPS. "I'll mark the location so we can find you again. Is six o'clock okay?"

"That sounds great," Jersey said.

"Well, I guess we'd better get back to work," Kate said, then extended her hand. "It was nice meeting you both."

"You too," Jersey said and gave Kate a firm handshake. Ed mumbled something indecipherable and also shook her hand, his eyes sliding off toward the right where the forest became dense and dark.

Kate couldn't help but follow his glance. She could barely see ten feet into the forest, but it looked like there might be some sort of cave just inside.

"What's that?" Kate asked.

Jersey whipped her head around to look in the direction. "Oh, that? That's nothing. We thought we found something there, but it turns out it was empty."

"Do you think it was a burial chamber?"

"That's what we were hoping." Jersey shook her head.

"But we were disappointed."

"I wonder if it had something to do with where they stored water?" Kate decided to embellish on her previous lie and make her quest sound more legitimate. "Did you find any evidence of containers or a hole lined with pottery shards?"

"No, nothing like that." Ed turned them toward the path they had come in on. "I assume you want to get back to where we met. Tony is putting the top of the pit back on, so you'll probably see him at the end of the path, but if he's already done be careful not to step in it."

"Yeah, we're not gonna fall for that again." Sal started down the path.

"You're not really going to tell her about any of our finds, are you?" Carlotta asked after they were out of hearing distance.

"Heck, no."

"Well, that hardly seems fair. She showed you what she found," Sal pointed out.

"Did she?" Kate looked back over her shoulder. "She was kind of secretive about that cave."

"You don't think she's with Markovic, do you?" Carlotta asked.

"No, probably not, but she might not be telling us everything."

"Well, you can hardly blame her on that. You weren't exactly straight with her, either," Sal said.

"Yeah, that's par for the course in the business." Kate poked at a fern with her walking stick.

"What's that saying?" Sal twisted his lips, then

snapped his fingers. "Keep your friends close, but your enemies closer."

Kate nodded. "All the more reason to join them for supper tonight."

CHAPTER FOURTEEN

They spent the rest of the afternoon exploring within the area they'd mapped out earlier. The tropical forest was dense and it was slow going, so they decided to call it quits around four p.m. after not finding a thing.

By the time they got back to the campsite, they were exhausted, sweaty, and feeling like they'd lost a pint of blood to the mosquitoes.

Kate had just changed out of the sweaty clothes she'd been wearing and into something more lightweight for supper when Vic and Benny came roaring out of the woods on two of the ATVs.

Vic gave Carlotta a peck on the cheek and then turned his eyes to Kate. "How'd you do, Kitten?"

"We had an interesting day. We didn't find much in

the way of Aztec tombs, but we did run across some archaeologists digging up a Mayan village."

Vic's left brow rose up a notch. "Really? Do you think that has something to do with the tomb we're looking for?"

"I don't think so. The Aztecs came after the Mayans. I don't think they used the same sites, but I guess anything is possible. Archaeologists are discovering new information all the time, so just because we've never found them to inhabit the same sites before doesn't mean it didn't happen."

"So is this person in competition with us?" Benny asked.

"Not according to what she told us. She's here excavating the Mayan site. She seems to be telling the truth and Gideon said her permits stated such. Anyway, they've invited us over for supper tonight. Maybe we can find out more."

"So Gideon knew about these other archaeologists?" Vic asked.

"Yes, he actually knows her personally,"

"Well, I guess she must be all right, then," Benny said.

"Did he have any other news?" Vic asked.

Kate chewed her bottom lip, remembering what Gideon had told her. "Unfortunately, Markovic must have uncovered some clues that have led him to this area. Gideon says he's dispatched a team to Mexico."

Vic's face darkened. "That's not good. He could really put a damper on our expedition. Do you think he knows where we are?"

Kate shook her head. "Not unless he has a contact like we did."

"Or better clues that lead right to this area." Gertie had walked out of the forest minutes earlier and caught the last part of the conversation.

"We'll have to really be on the lookout," Benny said. "His guys fight dirty."

Carlotta nodded, then turned to Vic. "And what did you guys find?"

"Well, we didn't find any relics or artifacts but we did stumble across a little village with a cantina."

Gertie's brows shot up. "So you spent the day drinking?"

"Not drinking," Benny said. "Well, we were drinking a little, but we had to in order to keep the locals talking about the tomb."

"And did you discover any new information?" Kate asked.

"As a matter of fact, we did. There *is* a tomb near here, but the people we talked to seemed very close-mouthed about it. Almost as if they were afraid." Vic said.

"That makes sense," Carlotta said. "The man in the market told Kate it was cursed, so that would be a legend locals were familiar with."

"Yeah, but I can't believe someone wouldn't have looted it by now. You know money trumps curses every time," Gertie said.

Benny frowned. "You see, that's the thing. The guys we talked to said someone *did* try to loot it many years ago. He was bitten by a snake in the process and his leg turned black and he died, after suffering for several weeks."

Kate shuddered. She knew there were poisonous snakes in the area and not all of them would kill you right away, but if you didn't tend to the bite, the poison would eat away at your tissue and cause just what Benny had described.

"I guess that pretty much scared everyone off," Vic said.

Carlotta scoffed. "Really? A snake bite here in the tropics hardly seems out of the ordinary. I think they were just being superstitious."

"Let's hope that's the case," Kate said. "They didn't happen to say where this tomb was located?"

Vic shook his head. "No one could say for sure. They just kept talking about curses and snakes and something about Itizuma's legend that is better off not being known."

Kate thought about the hookah man's words about how some things are better off left buried. She'd thought he was just referring to the curse, but from what Vic had just said, it sounded like there might be more to it."

"We might have found something." Gertie's words pulled Kate from her thoughts.

"Really?" Kate asked.

"We were just walking along when we stumbled on some flat stones. They had carvings. Most of them were hard to make out … except for this baby." Gertie held her cell phone out. On it was a picture of a rock with a carved creature. Kate bent forward to get a closer look, a feeling of foreboding running through her—the creature looked like part bird and part snake. She hoped there was no such creature in real life.

"That looks like Quetzalcoatl," Carlotta said. "It's like some sort of God. The feathered serpent. The feathers are said to represent the heavens and the wind and the snake the earth and fertility. It was an important Aztec God, so you might be on to something."

"Where did you find it?" Kate asked.

Gertie pulled out her GPS and they all looked over her shoulder. "Right in the corner of our search area." She pointed to a speck on the map on the GPS screen display.

"That's near the archaeological dig," Kate said.

"What an interesting coincidence," Vic added.

"Yeah, but it must be just that—a coincidence. I saw the relics they were digging and they looked too early for Aztec," Kate said. "And Jersey really seemed sincere, didn't she?"

Carlotta pressed her lips together. "She did, but it could be that *she* is sincere and someone else on her team isn't."

"You mean like a mole?" Kate asked. "Using her dig to gather information on the Aztec tomb?"

"Maybe. If that tomb really is somewhere near the Mayan ruins, they could be just biding their time and trying to find out what they can.'

"Kind of like what you guys will be doing at supper tonight?" Gertie asked.

Kate grimaced. "When you put it that way, it makes us sound like we're no better than Markovic's guys."

"I'm not sure about Jersey. She's too cute to be up to no good, but that Ed guy seemed awfully antagonistic," Sal said.

"Yeah, he wasn't very friendly," Kate agreed.

"It could be he's just wary of strangers stumbling on their dig. They have more reason to be suspicious of us then we are of them since they were here first," Vic pointed out.

"True dat." Sal rummaged in the khaki duffel bag and came up with a gallon bottle of rum. "But if they are up to something, I have a feeling it will all come out once I start fixing them up with my famous Pearl Harbors tonight at dinner."

CHAPTER FIFTEEN

Leave it to the *Golden Capers* gang to bring all the fixings for Pearl Harbors, Kate thought as she sipped one from a mason jar. To the left, a bonfire crackled. Shadows danced in its light as Benny regaled everyone with one of his many tales. Dinner had been fun, with both crews pitching in to provide a feast of steak, potatoes and asparagus.

Kate and Jersey had moved away from the fire. It was still in the eighties even at night and Kate liked the cooler air on the outskirts of the camp. Away from the fire, she could see the stars and hear the insects chirping.

Kate looked over her purple paper umbrella—yes, Gertie had even thought to bring drink umbrellas—at Jersey, who was seated beside her on the stone bench sipping her own drink.

"So how did you get interested in archaeology, anyway?" Kate asked.

"I guess you could say it's in my blood. My grandfather was an archaeologist so I was raised on it." Jersey took a small sip of her drink. "What about you?"

"I'm not an archaeologist, really. But my job at the museum takes me out in the field like this sometimes. To scout out things the museum might be interested in."

"Interesting job. Does Gideon do that, too?"

"Oh, no, he mostly stays back in the lab restoring paintings and doing research." Kate left out the part about his inventions. Sometimes it was better not to give too much information about their covert operations. "Did you know him well?"

Jersey tucked a strand of her long, blonde hair behind her ear. "Not really. We hung around with the same people in school."

"Oh." Kate looked down at her drink. It was almost gone while Jersey's was still three quarters full. Maybe she should slow down. She was starting to feel a bit giddy and she tended to talk too much when she drank.

Over at the campfire, the others were laughing and having a good old time. Except for Ed. Kate could see him lurking sullenly around the edges.

"What's with your associate, Ed? He doesn't seem like he wants us here." Ooops, maybe she shouldn't have said that out loud.

Jersey's lips twisted. "He can be kind of a party pooper. My boss insisted that he come along as my assistant, but the way he acts sometimes, I wonder if he thinks *he's* the one in charge."

"Who is your boss?"

"Oh, a private company." Jersey waved her hand dismissively. "Anyway, Ed's not all that bad. He's just really committed to the project and he's kind of straight-laced about it. Doesn't want anything to screw it up."

Kate decided it was probably better to move the conversation away from Ed. She wasn't sure she trusted the guy and it seemed like maybe Jersey didn't, either. Jersey seemed sincere and Kate believed she was just out there trying to recover what she could from the Mayan village. Kate couldn't help but wonder if maybe Ed had another agenda. But that wasn't Kate's problem.

"How long have you been out here?" Kate asked.

"Two months."

"Wow, don't you miss malls? Or anyone back home?"

Jersey's eyes darkened. "Malls, maybe. Someone at home, no. That's why I'm out here, actually. To forget about someone at home."

"Bad breakup?"

Jersey nodded. "The worst. We were engaged, and I thought things were perfect. I had visions of white picket fences and two point five kids … until I caught him with my best friend. They both betrayed me, so I figured I was better off in the jungle alone."

Kate's heart twisted in sympathy. She knew how that felt. She found herself pouring her own story about how she and Ace had been more than partners during her brief stint in the FBI. It had been wonderful—idyllic. For a while, she'd thought he was 'the one' but when she'd used unconventional means to catch a bad guy, he'd betrayed her to the FBI. The bad guy had gotten off the hook and Kate had lost her job. It had taken her a long time before she could even think about Ace Mason without wanting to shoot something. At least now she didn't feel so angry, but she still never wanted to see him again, even if he had tried to make up for it by saving her life last summer.

Jersey listened with a sympathetic ear. "Who needs them, anyway? We're better off now." She held her fist out for a knuckle tap.

Kate tapped Jersey's fist with her own. "That's for sure. "Kate couldn't ignore her bladder's nagging any longer. One can only drink so many Pearl Harbors before one needed a break. She stood up. "Excuse me. Nature calls."

Jersey's hand shot out. "I'll hold your drink."

Kate gave her the drink and walked off into the woods, venturing as far from the campsite as she felt comfortable. On the way back, she walked past the cave-like opening she'd seen when they'd been visiting earlier in the day.

Curiosity got the better of her. She hesitated in front of the cave, glancing quickly back at the campfire to see if anyone was watching. No one was. She stepped closer to get a better look. It looked like some sort of opening that had been cut down into the earth and shored up with rocks and timber. The inside was dark. Kate's curiosity warred with a sense of foreboding.

Should she go in?

Her heart skittered as she stepped forward. Her foot came down on a dry twig, the snapping sound echoing loudly in her ears. She took another tentative step forward, bringing her right foot up in the air, when a rustling just where she was about to land her foot startled her. She squeaked and fell backward, her eyes widening in surprise when someone caught her. She turned to see who it was, her heart freezing when she met the dark, menacing eyes of Ed.

"What are you doing out here?" he asked.

"Umm, I was just out on a nature call and I guess I got lost," Kate said lamely.

"It's dangerous in there. I thought we told you to stay away from here." As if to prove his point, Ed smacked the inside of the doorway with a stick. Kate heard the unmistakable slithering of snakes as they moved away from the noise.

Ed leaned toward her, so close she could feel his hot breath on her cheek. "This cave is full of snakes. Poisonous snakes."

"Sorry, I didn't realize. I'll be more careful next time." Kate pulled her arm away from him and started back toward the campsite.

She could feel his eyes burning a hole in her back as she walked away. When she was halfway to the camp, she couldn't resist looking back over her shoulder. Ed was still watching her, his arms crossed over his chest. She quickly turned and hurried back to the campfire, wondering what was more dangerous—the cave with the snakes or Ed.

CHAPTER SIXTEEN

Kate woke up the next morning with a pounding head and a feeling of trepidation. Maybe she shouldn't have had that second Pearl Harbor, she thought, as she crawled out of her sleeping bag and made her way toward the smell of fresh-perked coffee.

Carlotta, Vic, Gertie, Benny, Frankie and Sal were already sitting around the campfire. A cast iron skillet loaded with scrambled eggs sat on top of the stainless steel grill over one half of the fire. Crisp strips of bacon were laid out on a paper towel on the table.

"That smells divine." Kate didn't know which smelled better, the coffee or the bacon and eggs.

"Grab a plate. It's just ready now." Carlotta gestured to the stack of paper plates and Kate helped herself then grabbed a big cup of coffee and sunk into one of the camp chairs next to the fire.

"I think we're all in agreement that we she should check out the site that Gertie and Benny found," Vic said.

Kate nibbled the crispy end of a piece of bacon. "The one with the feathered serpent?"

"Yes."

"Definitely. That seems like our biggest lead. We'll map off the area and each take small quadrants." Kate looked at her watch. "And I need to remember to connect with Gideon at twelve thirty-five."

After breakfast, they looked up the coordinates on Gertie's GPS, then got on the ATVs and headed to the site. The area was thick with tropical foliage. Kate was glad she'd brought her walking stick which she tapped zealously on the leafy fronds so as to scare away any snakes that might be hiding inside.

The abundance of thick scrub plants made it difficult to map out areas for each of them to explore. They divided the area into quadrants—north, south, east and west—then made several sections in between. Kate took the west quadrant and proceeded to walk the area, slowly making her way back and forth looking for signs of ancient civilizations.

She'd made her way quite far from the others when she discovered a pile of rocks set in an unnatural pyre.

She fisted her walkie-talkie. "I think I have something."

"What have you got?" Vic's voice crackled over the walkie-talkie.

Kate flicked out the knife on the end of her walking stick and used it to cut away some of the surrounding plants. She found a rectangular slab like an old marker that had once been standing upright but had been toppled by centuries of forest growth. On it were the geometric carvings typical of the ancient Aztecs.

"I found some rocks in an unusual formation and near them some Aztec carvings," Kate said.

"We haven't found anything." Gertie's voice dripped with disappointment. "Maybe we should all converge in Kate's area and help her clear more of it away."

"That sounds like a good plan. The forest is very thick here and I could use some help clearing away the plants." Kate rattled off her coordinates. She whacked at more plants as she waited for them to arrive, which didn't take long since they were all only a few minutes away.

Kate showed them the marker and the stones, then they got to work clearing away enough of the plants to give them room to scout out any other signs of ancient civilization.

Even though the leaves on the taller trees provided a canopy of shade, the overhead sun beat down on them, causing Kate to sweat uncomfortably.

"That overhead sun really is hot." Carlotta echoed her thoughts.

"Yeah, it must be high noon or thereabouts," Benny said.

Kate's eyes flew to the watch on her wrist. "It's actually half past. The satellite is almost overhead. It's time to contact Gideon."

She moved to a more densely forested spot, sat down on a boulder and fiddled with the watch. After a few minutes, it crackled with static. Gideon's face appeared through a snowy, dotted haze.

"Kate, you look a little pale. Is everything okay?" Gideon asked.

"Well, it's hot as Hades here and I'm in the middle of the jungle getting eaten by mosquitoes," she snapped, then added, "and I may have stayed up a little late last night with your friend, Jersey."

Gideon frowned. "Jersey? You mean you ran into her?"

"Yes. You could say we stumbled into her." Kate glanced over at Carlotta and Sal who laughed at her joke. "It turns out she's excavating a Mayan village not too far from here."

"Is that so? How is she?"

"Fine. She seems very nice, though I'm not sure about her assistant. He didn't seem to be very pleased that we were in the area."

Gideon pursed his lips. "I guess that makes sense. You know how archaeologists are. They don't want anyone jumping claim on their find."

"Don't I know it," Kate said. "But I might have good news. She angled the watch toward the marker. "We just found this and we're searching the area to see if there's anything else. This is definitely Aztec, right?"

"Yes, it is."

"And Gertie found a carving yesterday with some sort of bird serpent on it."

"Quetzalcoatl? That was an Aztec deity or god. You guys could be onto something."

"Great. What about you? Have you made any progress with the painting?"

"As a matter of fact, I have. There does seem to be something under the top layer of paint but it's not a map or anything. It almost looks like some sort of a cipher for a code. It could be hieroglyphs, though. I can't make out a lot of it, but it looks like frogs."

"A code? What kind of code and how would that help us find the tomb?"

"I'm not sure. It might be a way to help you find the tomb or a way to help you with what's inside the tomb."

Kate's brows pinched together. "What do you mean help us with what's inside the tomb?"

Gideon shook his head. "I'm not sure but I get a funny feeling that Itizuma may have been more than just a ruler. He might have had some sort of valuable secret and it could be in his tomb."

Kate scoffed. "I highly doubt some secret from six hundred years ago would be of interest to anyone now."

"I wouldn't be too sure. This could be something pretty big from the rumblings I'm hearing. And even worse than that, I think Markovic might know more than we do. We don't know what was revealed in his half of the painting."

"Do you think this could have something to do with the curse?"

"It's possible. Or it's possible the curse was invented to keep people away from the tomb. Whatever is in there may be more valuable than gold or riches and a curse would be just the thing to keep superstitious locals at bay."

Kate remembered what the hookah man had told her. She thought it was just some legend that he was warning her about, a legend probably instilled long ago to keep people from raiding the tomb. But the way he had said it did seem a little strange, especially the part about how some things should stay buried.

A seed of the doubt rooted in Kate's stomach. From the very start, she'd thought Markovic's interest in the painting was a little odd. Sure, an Aztec tomb loaded with gold and ancient carvings could be worth a lot of money, but you can't just go into a tomb and take things out. You have to register with the government and you wouldn't get to keep everything. There *was* money to be made, but not as much as one might think.

But if there was something else—something more valuable than gold like Gideon had indicated, Kate needed to know about that right away. Because if there *was* something else, it could change the scope of her assignment. She needed to know what she was up against and there was only one way for her to find that out. She had to go back and talk to the hookah man.

CHAPTER SEVENTEEN

The market was the same as it had been when Kate had visited it two days before—the colorful fabrics, the smell of roasting meat and the lush fruits and vegetables. But she didn't have time to stop and look at any of it. She was on a mission. It was already late afternoon and she didn't want to be driving back to the campsite in the dark, so she hurried down the narrow aisles of the market looking for the indigo and white stall.

She cut down a side alley and the stall came into view. As she walked toward the hut, the curtain fluttered closed. She saw the hookah clatter to the ground and the man's feet stuck out under the curtain—toes up.

Kate's heart lurched. She ran to the stall, shoving the curtain aside, her gaze falling on the hookah man at her feet. In the back of the stall she was vaguely aware of a tall, blond man running out. Was it Snake Ring? The figure had looked familiar, but she couldn't tell for sure—he'd run out too fast.

Her brain whirred with indecision. She wanted to chase the tall blond, but the man at her feet needed her more. She turned her attention to the hookah man, who looked up at her with dying, blue eyes. She bent down to help him, her heart galloping in her chest.

How badly was he hurt? The spreading red stain on his chest seemed to indicate it was pretty bad and Kate found herself at a loss as to what to do.

He grabbed her wrist with a shaky hand. Kate's heart jerked when she noticed a tattoo on the underside of his wrist—a snake in a figure eight with its tail in its mouth—very similar to the icon Kate had found.

"Please … Please … " The man stuttered.

Kate grappled for her phone. "I'll call the police emergency."

"Too late." He let out a bubbling cough. "Stay away from that tomb. What is inside should never be revealed."

"What *is* inside?" Kate stared into his eyes, watching the light slowly fade. His mouth opened but all that came out was a wheezing sound and then his eyes went dark, his head lolled to one side.

He was dead.

"Damn!" Anger surged through Kate. She didn't know much about the man, but he'd been killed in cold blood. That made her mad. Judging by his last words, Kate knew his death was directly related to the tomb she was looking for. She had to find out why, and only one person could tell her that—the killer. Before she knew what she was doing, she was on her feet and running out the back of the tent in the direction the blond man had taken.

She skidded to a stop in the main aisle, looking around for the man. Luckily, he was tall and she recognized his head casually walking around several aisles over.

"Hey, you! Wait!" The man whipped his head around. It *was* Snake Ring! Kate took off after him, dodging around a cart of oranges and pushing a woman out of her way.

Snake Ring broke into a run. He pushed the produce stand over. Limes, oranges and grapefruit spilled out, bouncing and rolling across the street.

"Hey!" The vendor raised his fist at Snake Ring's back, but Snake Ring didn't slow down. He took a right and Kate put her head down and ran as fast as she could to catch up.

She turned down the same aisle but there was no sign of him.

"Shoot!" She paused, looking right and left. "Where the heck did he—"

A hand came out of a black curtain and clamped itself around her mouth, cutting off her words and dragging her inside a dark stall.

———

Kate twisted and thrashed to free herself from the strong arms that trapped her against a muscular torso. She tried to bite the hand, but it was clamped too tightly over her mouth. She stomped her heel on the assailant's foot.

"Ouch!"

The voice sounded familiar. Kate paused trying to place it.

"Stop struggling, for crying out loud. I'm on your side."

No. It couldn't be.

Kate reared back and jammed her elbow into her captor's stomach with all her might.

"Oomph!"

He let go and doubled over in pain. Kate turned to look at him, her suspicions confirmed. Her assailant was none other than her former partner, FBI agent Ace Mason.

Kate felt like kicking him where it counted, but she held herself back. "What are you doing attacking me?"

"I wasn't attacking you. I was saving you from getting into an altercation with Burgess Maxon."

"Who?"

"The man you were chasing. Burgess Maxon. He works for Markovic."

"I thought that was him. What is he doing here? And more importantly, what are *you* doing here?"

"What are *you* doing here?" Ace's gray eyes drilled into hers. She'd forgotten how disquieting those eyes could be. How it felt like they were looking right into your soul, making some sort of deep connection. She ripped her eyes away.

"I don't have to tell you what I'm doing here," she said.

"No, you don't, because I already know what you're doing here. I was just giving you a chance to tell me on your own." Ace pulled the edge of the curtain back slightly and peered out into the marketplace.

"What are you looking for? Is someone after you?" Kate asked.

"No, but someone might be after you."

"Why would someone be after me?"

Ace sighed and let the curtain drop. He stepped closer to her, which had the annoying effect of making her heartbeat kick up a notch. She hated that, so she took a step backwards.

"Listen, Kate, I know you don't want to hear this, but things could get pretty dangerous here."

"You mean because Markovic wants to find the same tomb as the *Ritzholdt Museum*?"

"There is a lot more to this than just finding a tomb," Ace said.

No kidding, Kate thought. Since when was the FBI interested in Aztec tombs? Never. Just the mere presence of Ace Mason indicated something more was going on. Not to mention the violent death of the hookah man. But what, *exactly*, was going on?

"Clearly," she said. "And what exactly is this about?"

"I wish I could tell you. But I really can't."

Ace's comment made Kate's blood boil over. It was just like him to go by the book. The information was probably on a 'need to know' basis and he figured she didn't *need to know*, even though clearly there was something going on here that could endanger her.

She narrowed her eyes. "You know what, Ace Mason? I don't need you here saving me from the bad guys. You obviously don't trust me enough to tell me what's going on and I can take care of myself."

She spun around to leave. Ace grabbed her arm, spinning her back to face him. He pulled her close.

"Kate, I'm serious. This is bigger than you think. And dangerous. I'm giving you this one warning to stop looking for the tomb and go home before something bad happens."

Kate jerked her arm away. "In case you've forgotten, I don't work for the FBI and I don't have to take orders from you anymore!"

She shoved the curtain open and stomped off into the marketplace, her blood simmering as she headed toward the Jeep.

How dare Ace try to warn her off!

If he thought she was going to meekly pack up and go home on his warning, he had another thing coming. If anything, it just made her more determined than ever to find that tomb and see what the heck was inside it that was worth killing for.

CHAPTER EIGHTEEN

You wouldn't believe what happened in the market!" Kate slammed the door of the Jeep, causing everyone at the campsite to look at her with startled eyes.

Vic's brows rose a notch. "Did you find out about Gideon's warning?"

"Not really." Kate fisted her hands on her hips. "The hookah man was dead. I think the killer was one of Markovic's guys. But that's not the worst part. The worst part was that I ran into Ace Mason and he tried to warn me off from finding the tomb."

Vic's brows rose another notch. "Why would the FBI be interested in the tomb?"

"You tell me," Kate said. "It's probably just Ace Mason trying to wield his power."

Carlotta leveled a look at her. "You don't really think

that, do you? If Ace is warning you off, I think there's something to it. Maybe you need to put your personal feelings aside and look at this objectively."

Kate sank down in one of the chairs, feeling deflated. Her mother was right. Her anger at Ace went beyond his warning on this project. She didn't want to be so pig-headed about him that she put everyone in danger, but she still wasn't going to quit looking for the tomb.

"I guess you're right. But what could there possibly be in an ancient tomb that the FBI thinks is dangerous?" Kate asked.

"That's what we need to find out," Gertie said. "Did you say that your contact there was dead?"

Kate nodded. "I saw the killer go out the back and chased him. That's when Ace intercepted me. He said the killer was one of Markovic's guys and I thought I recognized him as being the guy who was in the muse-um when we stole back the painting. And he's also one of the guys who was at Estelle's."

Sal frowned. "That's not a good sign. That must mean that Markovic is on your trail and that the hookah man had some interesting information. He probably told him we were camped out here."

Kate felt a pang of sadness at the thought of the hoo-kah man. When she'd stormed by his stall after talking to Ace, she'd seen the police there. They had been looking around inside the stall, the medical examiner examining the body. She knew there was nothing she could have done for the man but she still felt kind of like a heel for taking off and leaving him there, even though he was already dead. Thankfully, no one had seen her or she'd probably have the police out looking for her as a person of interest.

"Well, thankfully that guy didn't know exactly where we camped. He just gave us vague directions," Carlotta said.

"Yeah, but Markovic has the other half of that painting which might lead him to a more specific location than our half of the painting. Our half got us to this camp here, but the Aztec artifacts we're finding are quite a ways away from here," Bennie pointed out.

Kate heard a whirring noise behind her and looked over to see Sal working a white, frothy drink in what looked like some sort of makeshift blender.

"What are you doing?" she asked.

Sal looked up sheepishly. "I finally found a good use for that little motor gizmo Gideon put in the heels of our boots." Sal tipped the glass toward her and took a sip. "This is a pina colada. Bottoms up."

Kate remembered she had a motor gizmo in her boot, too, along with the other gadgets Gideon had given her. She'd barely paid attention when he'd showed them to her in the lab. She thought about the necklace, earrings and bracelet that snapped together to form a digging tool. Maybe she should wear those, just in case. With Markovic's guys on their tail, you never knew what might come in handy and Gideon had already lectured her about not wearing them—'you never know when those might get you out of trouble,' he'd said.

Kate's thoughts turned to practical matters. "So what do you guys think we should do?"

"Well, I don't know about you people, but I've never

been afraid of a little danger," Gertie scoffed.

Sal scrunched up his face. "Me, either."

Benny choked out a laugh. "We've dealt with people much worse than Markovic in our day."

"And we've all outsmarted the FBI," Carlotta added, eliciting a laugh from the entire group.

"So, you all agree that we should continue looking for the tomb, then?" Kate asked.

"Yes," Vic said. The others nodded their heads. "Maybe we should even move camp up near where we found that snake symbol."

"That's a good idea. I plugged everything into the GPS and I have a little map here." Gertie motioned for them to look over her shoulder at the tablet she held in her hand.

From Gertie's map, Kate could see their current camp in relation to where they'd found the feathered snake icon and the obelisk from earlier that morning. Even closer to the area where they'd been earlier was another spot that Gertie had marked.

"What's that?" Kate pointed to the other mark.

"Oh, that?" Gertie said. "My tracker put in the coordinates from everywhere we've been. "That site right there is where we were last night. It's the site of Jersey's camp."

―――――

They decided to move camp the next day as it was too late at night to move by the time they'd assessed all their information. Kate spent a restless night, half expecting to be awakened with an alert that the bad guys were coming. But she was not awakened in the middle of the night and the next morning they pulled up stakes and moved north, closer to the Aztec site.

They found a fairly open area near a stream where they decided to camp out. From there, it was a short walk to where Kate had found the marker. They needed to do a wider search of the area and the camp was centrally located.

"Do you think it's a coincidence that Jersey's dig is near here?" Carlotta asked as she turned on the propane grill to make coffee after they had set up the tents.

Kate pressed her lips together. "I'm not sure. It's possible the Aztecs built their village utilizing some of the structures of the Mayans. I've not heard of that before, but I'm no expert and I guess anything is possible."

"But what does that mean to our project?" Gertie asked. "Do we have to share with Jersey?"

Kate shrugged. "I wouldn't mind sharing with Jersey, but her assistant Ed is another matter. He seemed downright hostile to me when we were there the other night."

"You mean when you tried to sneak into that cave that you weren't supposed to go in?" Carlotta's lips quirked in a smile.

Kate dipped her head. "Yeah. I guess I kind of had it coming, but he could've been nicer about it.

"Anyway, from what I can tell, our job is just to find the tomb," Carlotta said. "Then Max will have to get the appropriate permissions and send a team out to excavate it. So, I imagine he'll be the one who has to deal with Jersey if there are any disputes about the area."

Kate nodded. "Right. It's not really anything we need to worry about. We just need to *find* the darn tomb." Now that so many people were after it, Kate's desire to be the one to find it had ratcheted up tenfold.

"Maybe we should at least warn her about Markovic's guys, though," Carlotta suggested.

Kate's top teeth worried her bottom lip. "That's a good idea. Those guys are real bad-asses, and if they stumble across her dig and think she's onto the Aztec tomb, they'd have no qualms about hurting her." Kate shuddered, remembering the sting of the poison dart in her neck.

"But how do we warn her without tipping her off that we're not just here looking for ancient water reservoirs?" Benny asked.

"We could just say that we'd gotten word about some violent poachers in the area," Vic suggested. "They already know those kinds of people are around, otherwise they wouldn't have dug those pits like the one you guys fell into."

"Yeah." Sal rubbed his elbow. "I still have some pain in my elbow from that fall. I say Jersey can take care of herself. No warning needed."

Kate wrestled with her conscience. On the one hand, she didn't want Jersey to suspect that they were onto anything more important than looking for evidence of an old Mayan water system. That was certainly nothing that poachers or bad guys would be interested in. On the other hand, she had developed a fondness for Jersey. She felt like they had bonded the other night and she hated the thought of Snake Ring shooting her with the poison dart ... or worse.

Not to mention that she felt like she should probably take another look at Jersey's artifacts. If the Aztec site was so close to the Mayan site, there may be some correlation. Jersey might have stumbled across something that could help Kate.

"I don't want to let on what our real project is," Kate said. "But, it would be the neighborly thing to do to warn her that we know somebody nasty is in the area. I think we should take a trip over there to give her the warning and see if we can find out anything more about the connection between her Mayan village and our Aztec tomb."

CHAPTER NINETEEN

Jersey was bent over the artifacts table when Kate and Gertie got to her site. As they approached her, she whirled around. Then, upon seeing it was Kate and Gertie, gave a nervous laugh.

"I thought I heard something behind me. You startled me," she said.

"Sorry about that." Kate jerked her chin toward the table. "Did you guys come up with some new finds?"

"What? Oh, no … I was just looking over what we had." Jersey narrowed her eyes at Kate. "So, what brings you here?"

"Well, I actually came with kind of a warning. According to Gideon, there's some really bad poachers in the area."

"Oh? We deal with poachers all the time. Is there something special about these guys?"

"Gideon says they're quite ruthless. I just wanted to come and warn you so you could be on extra alert," Kate said. "Did you hear anything about poachers from the people you're working for?"

Jersey's eyes slid toward the camp. Ed was just coming out of his tent. Kate saw his eyes darken when he noticed them. He changed direction and headed their way.

"I haven't heard anything. Ed's usually the one who communicates with them, but as you know, communication out here can be pretty spotty. I'm not sure if he's talked to them recently," Jersey said.

Kate shrugged. "They may not know. The *Ritzholdt* was watching this particular group and that's how I found out."

Jersey's brows ticked up. "Oh. Well, thanks for letting me know. I really appreciate that. We'll be sure to be extra watchful."

"What's going on?" Ed glanced from Jersey to Kate.

"Kate was nice enough to bring us a warning about some poachers in the area," Jersey said.

"Yeah? We appreciate that." Ed looked at Kate. He didn't seem appreciative. He glanced at the artifact table. "I think we'd better start packing up these finds."

"Have you heard anything about any artifact thieves in the area?" Gertie quizzed Ed.

"No. We haven't talked to the home base," he said.

"We've been busy digging," Jersey added.

"Speaking of which…" Ed flipped his wrist over to look at his watch which he wore with the face on the inside. Kate struggled to keep from gasping when she recognized a tattoo peeking out from under his wide watch band—a snake in a figure eight. "We'd better get going. We have a deadline to meet."

"He's right." Jersey put her arms around Kate and Gertie's shoulders, turning them around and sweeping them out of the tent. "Were taking a trip into town on Friday to get some of this shipped out. Our backers are very anxious and we need to recover some more artifacts so we are under a tight deadline. But I really do appreciate you guys coming by. Maybe we could get together for dinner again?"

"That sounds like fun," Kate said. Jersey started escorting them toward the small path that ended in the pit Kate had fallen into when they'd first met, but Kate stopped her and turned toward another path.

"We moved camp. It's in that direction now." She pointed toward the narrow path she and Gertie had come in on.

Jersey's face scrunched up. "Really? Why did you move?"

Kate hesitated. She realized too late that she hadn't thought up a sufficient lie.

"We found what we think were some water reservoirs that we wanted to explore further." Gertie saved her. "We figured it would be better if our camp was closer. Speaking of which, we'd better get back. Right, Kate?"

"Right. We'll see you soon." Kate waved to Jersey, and then turned and started down the path they'd come in on.

When they'd walked for a little ways, Kate heard a slithery sound behind her. She whirled around, whacking at a plant with her walking stick. Nothing was in the plant. She heard the sound again but realized it was further back.

"Did you hear that?" Kate asked.

Gertie, who had gotten a few steps ahead of her, stopped and cocked her head sideways. She listened for a few seconds and shook her head. "I didn't hear anything."

Kate shrugged. "Must be my imagination. I thought I heard something back there."

"Probably just a monkey," Gertie said. "This jungle is full of them, you know."

"I know." Kate glanced uneasily behind her, remembering the tattoo on Ed's wrist. Coincidence? Or did Ed have a connection to the hookah man? And if so, what did it mean? Snake Ring had killed the hookah man, but why? And if Snake Ring was an enemy of the hookah man, did that mean he was an enemy of Ed? Would that make Ed her ally?

Vic's voice crackled through the walkie-talkie clipped to Kate's belt. "Where are you guys?"

Kate picked up the little device and pressed the button. "We're just heading back from Jersey's site now."

"Get a move on. I think we found something significant."

CHAPTER
TWENTY

Kate was surprised at the amount of work they'd done in the short time she'd been gone. The five of them had managed to clear out an area that must have been twenty feet wide. They were standing in a cluster, pointing at something on the ground.

Kate felt the excitement bubble up in her chest as she got closer. "What is it? What did you find?"

They stepped aside to reveal two columns of stone about knee height. The tops were jagged as if the stones had broken off. They were no ordinary stones. Kate could see they were carved with symbols.

"It looks like this used to be some sort of archway." Carlotta pointed to a heap of what looked like vine-covered logs that lay strewn to the left. "I think this is the rest of the sides and the top. They must've collapsed and fallen over sometime during the last six hundred years."

Kate bent over to inspect them. Carlotta was right. They weren't logs as they'd first appeared. They were stone—the same type of limestone the jagged columns were made out of.

She pulled on the vines that clung to the sides and revealed some of the stone below which had the same etchings as the columns. A closer look revealed that they appeared to be a bunch of winged frogs hopping in a line. In between the frogs were geometric carvings.

"This is great. Do you think the archway leads to something?" Kate peered into the dense forest behind the broken columns of the archway.

"That's what we were thinking." Benny stepped backwards, away from the two posts sticking out of the ground. He looked up at the sky. "If this was a complete archway you could see that the sun would line up directly in the center and show through it at a certain time of day."

Kate stood next to him and glanced at her watch. It was eleven forty-five and the sun was just to the left of the archway. "Looks like it would line up at just about high noon," she said.

"I'd be more interested to see what the archway leads to." Gertie took several paces past the archway and shaded her eyes to peer into the forest. "It looks like there's a mound in there."

"We should clear the rest of this out," Kate said.

They all got to work with their various tools, clearing the dense vegetation. Kate was in the front, swinging her walking stick like a sickle.

Clonk.

Instead of the soft, yielding vegetation she was expecting, her stick hit something hard at the very base of the hill. Stone. "I think there's a rock here."

Sal came over with a small shovel and tried to pry up the rock to get it out of the way. He tossed the rock aside and Kate noticed it had an unnatural, squarish appearance.

"Wait a minute. That's no ordinary rock." Kate bent down and brushed off the thick, green moss that covered the rock. The rock looked like it had been chiseled but not recently—more like hundreds of years ago. She took a step back and looked at the hill, noticing for the first time it was pyramid-shaped.

Gertie stood beside her and noticed at the same time. "That's no hill. That there is a pyramid."

A ripple of excitement ran through them and they all got busy uncovering the bottom layer of stones. Kate could see that the pyramid had collapsed in on itself in several areas where the ground had sunken. This 'mound' was no natural object. It was manmade.

"It's definitely a pyramid, but probably not a tomb," Vic said. "It's not hollow."

"The Aztecs didn't have pyramids like the Egyptians. Not that we know of, anyway. They built theirs on mounds of dirt and faced them in stone," Benny said, surprising them all with his knowledge.

"But it's still exciting. And if I'm not mistaken, these symbols here," Sal pointed to one of the stones, "are Aztec, not Mayan. So this is our first indication that we're on the right path."

"This could be the beginning of the Aztec settlement.

We could be very near the tomb," Vic added.

"Yeah, but which direction is it in?" Kate asked. She remembered how she had thought someone was following them. Markovic's people could be hiding in the woods, just waiting for them to discover the tomb so they could then pounce on them, kill them and take everything for themselves.

They needed a map, something that would point them toward the location of the tomb quickly. If they fiddled around out here for much longer, they risked losing everything to the bad guys.

Her watch made static noises and Kate realized it was time for her to communicate with Gideon. She sat on the bottom ledge of the pyramid, took out one of the hard brushes Gideon had supplied her from her vest pocket and started scrubbing the moss and vines from the stone to see if there were any carvings.

"You there?" Gideon's voice blared out of her watch.

Kate worked the brush with her right hand and looked at the watch on her left. "I am and I think I might have something exciting to report."

"Me, too. You go first. But first, have you had any trouble with Markovic?"

Kate's gut churned. "He hasn't bothered us out here, but I have some bad news about your contact. He's been killed. And one of Markovic's men is the killer."

Gideon's mouth tightened. "That's not good. He might have gotten the same information you have and could be on to you right now."

Kate brushed away the thoughts of someone following them. "And that's not all. I ran into Ace Mason back in the market where your contact was."

Gideon's mouth got even tighter. "Really? So *that's* why he was asking so many questions. What's his interest in this?"

"I was hoping you could tell *me*. He tried to warn me off from looking for the tomb."

"That doesn't sound like something that the FBI would do."

Gertie, who had been standing beside her, cut in. "Like I said before, maybe our friend Ace is moonlighting. Maybe he wants to take the treasure for himself and set up a little retirement plan. I hear the FBI doesn't have that great of a pension."

Kate thought about this, but it didn't fit. Ace was a by-the-book kind of guy. She'd found that out the hard way. There had to be more to it, but she had no idea what it could be. "I don't think so. For some reason, the FBI is interested in this tomb. Ace alluded to there being more to it than just treasure. He made it sound like Itizuma had some secret that the FBI didn't want to get out."

Gertie scoffed. "What could some guy possibly have known six hundred years ago that could be important the FBI now?"

"That's a good question," Gideon said. "In fact, you may not be far off, though. I've done some research on the archaeologist this painting came from. Reginald White. His disappearance thirty years ago was very mysterious. He disappeared right from the archaeological dig in Mexico. But before that, there was quite a bit of press. He said he was working on recovering something that would stun the world. I have an old picture of his press conference somewhere. It's on site and I wondered if you might recognize the area. It could give you a clue to where the tomb is. But first, I wanted to tell you that I've discovered more under the painting."

That caught Kate's attention. She glanced at the watch face, the brush in her hand poised motionless over the stone. "Oh?"

"Yes, it seems there is a map of sorts. It's all symbols, but I think it might lead to the tomb. Of course, you need a reference point to follow it."

"Reference point?"

"Yes. On the map, it shows a frog-like creature."

Kate's heart skittered in her chest. "Wait a minute. I think we have that here." She ran over to the columns and put the watch camera up to show him. "Like this?"

"Sort of. I'll download a picture of it to your watch, but I'm afraid it might not help," Gideon said.

"Why not?"

"We only have one part of the map. The rest of it must be behind the half of the painting that Markovic has."

"And that's why he's here. He either knows how to get to the tomb or needs the other half of the map from me."

"Right. I downloaded the map and the picture of Reginald White's press conference. Maybe his location will give you a clue. The article says it was near his dig."

Kate looked at the watch. The display showed a middle-aged man, presumably Reginald White. He was gray-haired and wearing a white suit. Kate frowned at the scene. It looked very similar to where they were right now. Her eyes drifted over to the man standing with him.

Her heart jerked. That man was the spitting image of Jersey's assistant, Ed.

"Who's that with him?" she asked.

"Let me see … it says here it's his assistant. Ronald Raines. Why do you ask?"

"Because that guy is the spitting image of Jersey's assistant. I knew there was something weird about that guy!" Kate looked up in excitement.

"Wait a minute," Gideon said. "The guy in the picture couldn't be her assistant. This picture is thirty years old. He'd be an old man by now."

"Oh, I guess you're right. Ed is only in his mid-thirties. It couldn't be *him* but maybe it's one of his relatives. Maybe Ed had a grandfather who worked with Reginald White. That grandfather might've told Ed what they were on to and that's why he's insinuated himself in Jersey's project."

"You think Ed plans to use Jersey's work to help him get to the tomb and steal everything for himself?" Gideon asked.

"That's right." Kate felt vindicated. She knew there was a reason she didn't trust Ed. Then her thoughts turned dark. Ed was obviously unscrupulous, and poor Jersey trusted him and had no idea what he might do to her. "I'd better go warn Jersey right away!"

CHAPTER TWENTY-ONE

Kate ran all the way to Jersey's site, hoping to catch her before she went off to dig. She didn't know exactly where they were digging, but if Jersey wasn't at the campsite, she could at least leave a note.

In her haste, she almost forgot about the threat of snakes, barely swishing her stick as she ran. She was so focused on getting to Jersey that she was practically oblivious to the sounds behind her, until she thought she saw trees moving off to the side. Her first thought was that it could be Ed. Maybe he was onto her and trying to head her off before she got to Jersey. The thought only made her run faster, her heart pounding in her chest.

She burst into the clearing of Jersey's camp. It was empty! Then a movement over near the snake cave caught her eye. It was Jersey! Kate sprinted over.

"I'm glad I caught you!" Kate bent at the waist, her hands on her knees, and sucked in a breath.

Jersey's brow creased. "What is it? What's wrong?"

Kate took a few breaths, her hand pressing against the stitch in her side. "I need to warn you about your assistant."

Jersey glanced around the empty camp. "Ed?"

"Yes. I don't think he is what he seems to be."

"Really?" Jersey looked at her skeptically. "Why do you say that?"

"I saw a picture—"

"Shhh…" Jersey put out her hand to shush Kate, her eyes drifting out to the edge of the campsite. "Did you hear something?"

Kate wondered if it was Ed skulking around the edges of the camp and listening to them. Her hands snuck into her vest pocket, her stomach sinking when she realized she'd run off so fast that she'd forgotten to bring her gun. The only weapon she had was her walking stick. She felt grateful that Gideon had equipped it with a knife and she had the appropriate fencing skills, but it was still no match for a gun.

Luckily, Jersey *did* have a gun and she was holding it in her hand now. Leaves rustled behind them and Jersey motioned for Kate to go to one side of the cave while Jersey covered her with the gun.

"Hold it right there!" Kate whirled around to see Snake Ring and Onion Mole standing at the edge of the forest.

"You!" Kate gasped.

"So, we meet again." Snake Ring smirked. "This time,

you might not get off so easy."

Kate glanced around in a panic. Jersey had her gun on Onion Mole, but Snake Ring had his gun on Kate. All Kate had was a walking stick. And to make matters worse, she heard a slithering sound near the cave to her left. She slid her eyes to the left, her stomach turning inside out when she saw the unmistakable red and black stripes of a poisonous coral snake. A salty bead of sweat dripped into her eye and she blinked furiously to clear her vision.

"Looks like we're at a stalemate," Jersey announced.

Snake Ring jerked his gun in Kate's direction. "Just hand over your half of the map and I'll let you go."

"Map?" Jersey looked from Snake Ring to Kate.

"It's not really a map, per se," Kate explained. "It's just part of a painting. And I don't have it with me."

Kate was distracted by the slithering sound behind her. Was the snake getting closer? She angled her walking stick in the direction of the snake, ready to spear it should it venture any closer.

"Then you will take me to it." Snake Ring glanced at Onion Mole. "Get her!"

Onion Mole lunged toward Kate. At the same time, Kate swung her walking stick back toward the snake. She managed to hook the end of the stick under the snake and then flung it toward Onion Mole.

Onion Mole's hands flew up to ward off the flying reptile. The snake landed on his shoulder and slithered around his neck.

"Get it off!" Onion Mole twisted around, flailing his arms in an attempt to throw the snake off. He stumbled around, then blundered off blindly into the woods, the snake still curled around him.

Jersey trained her gun on Snake Ring. "Give it up. My partner will be back any minute and you'll be greatly outnumbered."

The thought of Ed coming back any minute didn't make Kate feel any safer, but she kept her mouth shut.

Snake Ring kept his eye on Jersey as he inched his way closer to Kate until he was within an arm's distance. "You wouldn't pull the trigger," he taunted Jersey.

Jersey answered him by clicking off the safety.

Snake Ring faltered and Kate seized the advantage. She pressed the button on the handle of her walking stick and the razor-sharp knife flicked out of the end. At the same time, she swooped it toward Snake Ring, lashing a bloody gash in his thigh.

"Ouch!" He looked down, his gun hand wavering while his free hand flew to the gash.

Jersey took her shot.

Snake Ring fell to the ground, a red stain spreading rapidly in the middle of his chest.

Kate looked at Snake Ring in astonishment.

"Wow. Thanks," she said, her heart swelling with the warmth of friendship.

"You're welcome," Jersey replied so matter-of-factly that Kate got the uneasy impression this wasn't the first person Jersey had shot. She seemed awfully at ease for someone who had just killed another person.

Kate felt a rush of euphoria, the kind you get when you've just escaped being shot by a creepy bad guy. It was especially sweet that she and Jersey had done it together. Girl power.

"Ha! We showed them." Kate slapped Jersey an enthusiastic high-five.

Jersey walked over to Snake Ring's body and turned him over with her foot. He had fallen right in front of the opening to the snake cave and Kate stood in between his body and the cave opening.

Jersey looked over the body at Kate. "Who is this guy?"

"He's one of the bad guys I warned you about," Kate said.

"And what was this business about a map?" Jersey asked.

Kate decided she'd better come clean. She didn't want to lie to Jersey, especially since the woman had just saved her life. Max might not like that she had told her about the Aztec tomb or that they might have to share the find, but it was the right thing to do.

Kate was trying to figure out how to break it to Jersey without sounding like a jerk when she noticed a piece of paper sticking out of the pocket of Snake Ring's cargo pants.

"What's this?" She bent down and took it out of his pocket. She opened it and her heart skittered with excitement. It was the other half of the map from underneath the painting.

"This is it!" The words slipped out and she realized Jersey would have no idea what they meant.

Click.

"Good, then hand it over."

"What?" Kate's brows mashed together. She looked up to see Jersey aiming the gun at her. "What are you doing?"

"I'll take that map," Jersey said.

Suddenly Jersey's kind blue eyes and girl-next-door face turned menacing. Kate clutched the map to her chest. "What do *you* want with this?"

"You're not very smart, are you?" Jersey asked and then, not waiting for an answer, continued, "You think I'm really here to excavate this Mayan ruin? I saw through you the first time you came to the camp. I know you're after the tomb of Itizuma and so am I."

"So this Mayan village dig is just a cover?" Kate asked incredulously.

Jersey laughed. "You got it. Now hand over the map." She stepped closer until the gun was only inches from Kate's forehead.

Kate stepped backward, which put her inside the snake cave. The sound of hissing in the dark recesses of the cave chilled her blood and Kate just stood there, frozen like an idiot while Jersey grabbed the map out of her hand.

"Thanks," Jersey said brightly as she stepped back out of the cave, the sunlight streaming over her blonde hair. Too bad she still had the gun pointed at Kate. Judging by the way she'd just shot Snake Ring, she had no qualms about shooting people and, at this range, she probably wasn't going to miss.

Behind Kate, the snakes hissed. She opened her mouth to try to talk some sense into Jersey. Maybe she could bargain with her, try to get her to team up with them or talk her way out of it. But no words came out. She was frozen, just like she had been in Stockholm and the steam tunnel.

Jersey folded the map and put it in her pocket. She squared her stance, her feet shoulder-width apart, both hands on the gun as she took aim.

Kate squeezed her eyes shut.

"Boom!"

The gun went off, but Kate didn't feel the piercing bullet tear through her flesh. Instead, she heard a rumble. Her eyes flew open and she saw an avalanche of rocks come down from the top of the mouth of the cave, sealing it off and leaving her in total darkness.

CHAPTER TWENTY-TWO

Being shot was preferable to being in a pitch black cave filled with snakes. But Kate hadn't been shot. She stood still, her heart thudding against her rib cage as her nostrils clogged with the smell of dank, moist dirt and her ears buzzed with the slithering, hissing sounds of the snakes.

How many snakes were in here? She couldn't tell.

There was one way to find out, though Kate wasn't convinced she wanted to. She stuck her trembling hand in her vest pocket in search of her phone. There was no cell phone reception, but she carried it with her anyway in case she needed to take pictures, and it just so happened she had a flashlight app on the phone.

She found the phone in her upper left pocket and pulled it out. Her fingers shook so badly she could barely press the button. She managed to find the app and then got her walking stick into snake-stabbing position in front of her before she dared turn it on.

She pressed the button and a stream of light splashed against the end of the cave. Kate whooshed out a breath when she realized it wasn't loaded with dozens of snakes as she had imagined. She slowly played the light along the sides, floor and top of the small cave. She could see the cave was not natural but rather had been built by humans many years ago—probably by the Mayans or the Aztecs. She didn't know how many layers of rock had blocked the entrance, but she could see no pinpricks of light coming through.

Should she try to dig her way out?

The light caught movement in the corner and her stomach twisted. Slowly, she aimed her beam at the corner, relief flooding through her when she saw there was only one snake. One *big* snake. It was probably twelve feet long and six inches thick in the middle.

The snake twisted around itself in a coiling mass of scales. Kate felt woozy. It looked at her with its golden, slitted eyes and she almost froze up again. But she couldn't let herself freeze this time—not if she wanted to get out of there.

But first, she needed to get rid of the snake. She slowly angled her arm back and then in one swift move, she flung the walking stick like a javelin toward the snake.

"Twanggg!"

The stick hit its mark, the blade slicing into the side of the furious reptile who coiled around itself, whipping it's body back and forth in an angry, hissing mass. Kate's heart stopped as she watched the blade fall out of the snake. It turned an angry gold eye on her, then disappeared through a tiny hole in the wall.

Kate's knees collapsed and she fell on the floor. She sat on the damp earth for several minutes, waiting for her heartbeat to return to normal and contemplating her next move.

She was alone in the cave, which was preferable to being with the snake, but Kate wondered if it would come back or if there would be others. Ed had said the cave was loaded with them and she didn't really want to stick around to find out. She felt a small spark of pride that she hadn't frozen on the spot like she had in the past. That knowledge flooded her with bravery and the courage gave her hope that she could find out way out of this.

She retrieved the walking stick. The blade had lodged into the dirt wall of the cave and as she pulled it out, she heard another hissing sound.

Her heart froze.

No, that wasn't hissing … it was running water. Shining the light on the area from where she'd just pulled the knife, Kate saw that it wasn't solid earth behind there … there was an empty space behind the wall.

Hope bubbled up in Kate's chest. That empty space could be a passageway that might lead out.

She poked her finger through the hole. The wall was about five inches thick, but it was solid and compact, as hard as cement. Digging a hole with the knife would take forever—she needed something faster. She looked around the cave, but it was empty.

"Damn!" Why couldn't there be an old shovel or something tossed in here like in the movies. And then it came to her.

She'd put on the clunky jewelry gadgets Gideon had given her earlier that morning so he wouldn't lecture her on their call and that was going to pay off in spades.

Saying a silent prayer of thanks to her lab rat friend, she tore off the necklace, bracelet and earrings and screwed the pieces together, the smaller pieces at one end graduating to the larger piece to make one big drill bit. Balancing her cell phone light on her lap, she opened the secret compartment in the heel of her boot and took out the motor, then attached it to the end of the drill bit.

Satisfied it was all together tightly, she held her breath and pressed the button. The drill worked perfectly.

It wasn't as good as a spade, but it would do in a pinch. It would certainly be faster than trying to dig through with the knife. She aimed it at the wall starting at waist height and drilled a series of holes, punching the dirt out in between and praying the wall did not collapse on top of her.

As the opening got larger, she could hear running water and smell the ozone-heavy air. Her heart thudded with excitement and she drilled faster. When the opening was big enough, she crouched down and crab-walked through.

The first thing she did on the other side was scan for snakes. Thankfully, there were none. She was in a long tunnel with a narrow river running down the side. By instinct, she knew that she should follow the water and it would eventually lead out. But how far would she have to go?

Glancing around, she didn't see any other way. The only other thing she could do was to try to dig out the rocks that had collapsed the mouth of the cave and if she did that, would Jersey be waiting on the other side with a gun?

No, her best bet was to follow this tunnel. She aimed the beam of her cell phone at the ground in front of her and started walking.

————

Kate had been walking for a tense five minutes when the tunnel started getting narrower, the ceiling lower. The river veered off to the right and then disappeared underground. Panic spread in Kate's chest. What if the tunnel she'd been following just ended here?

But it didn't. It took a sharp right into a cave-like room. The room smelled like musty old dirt. It had shelves all around and at first, the contents of the room didn't register.

But when they did, Kate gasped.

The room was full of human bones.

Kate instinctively pulled back from the sides, standing in the middle of the room. The bones were piled up on the shelves that had been cut into the earth at various levels around the sides of the room. Skulls, femurs, spines. It was creepy. But definitely better than snakes.

At the opposite end of the room, Kate realized some

of the skulls had been decorated. One was studded in turquoise tiles. One had carvings all over it. Some of those carvings looked familiar.

She went to the skull with the carvings, bending over and aiming her flashlight app at it. Her nerves tingled with excitement when she saw the familiar figure eight snake carving. This snake was very detailed and even had little feathers along its body, similar to the carving Gertie had found. Even more exciting were the winged frogs on either side—the same ones that were on the archway they'd found that morning. And if she wasn't mistaken, the frogs were marching off in a path that almost looked like a map.

Could this be the map to the tomb?

Kate wasn't about to pick the skull up and bring it with her. She did the next best thing and snapped a few pictures with her cell phone. When she finished, she looked for the exit, her excitement at finding the skull waning when she realized there was no exit. She'd hit a dead end.

Clink. Clink. Clink.

What was that noise?

Kate leaned closer to the skull. Was the noise coming from the skull?

Clink. Clink.

It was coming from the wall behind the skull, which Kate noticed wasn't dirt as she'd suspected before but solid stone. Was there another room behind there?

Kate ran her fingers along the wall and found a crack. It was thin, but she could feel cool air coming through it. Fresh air. The room on the other side could be her only way out.

As she pressed on the wall, she realized it wasn't a crack at all, but the opening in a false wall. She leaned her shoulder against it and it moved slightly. Would it slide open and give her access to the fresh air and possible exit on the other side?

But someone or *something* was on the other side making those clinking noises and all she had for a weapon was her walking stick. Maybe that was enough, though. She pressed the button on the handle and the knife slid out with an almost imperceptible click.

Her muscles tensed while she slowly pushed the wall open just enough for her to squeeze through.

Kate jumped into the room, positioned for battle, the blade held out in front of her as a weapon. "Hands in the air!"

The figure that had been bent over something on the other side of the room spun around. "Kate?"

"Ace?"

"What are you doing here?" He glanced at her walking stick. "Put that thing down."

Kate's eyes slid from Ace's face to where he had been crouched in the corner. It looked like he'd been chiseling away at some kind of rock on one of the walls. She put the stick down. "What are you doing here?" She gestured toward the stone.

"Making good use of my time." Ace pointed to something behind Kate and she turned around, for the first time realizing that the cave wasn't in complete darkness.

It was lit by sunlight that was coming in from something down at the end of a tunnel.

Hope flooded Kate's chest. "Is that the way out?"

"I don't know about that," Ace said. "It was certainly the way in. But you can't get out that way. It's too high up."

"Too high up?" Kate started at him, confused for a second before realizing what he was talking about. "You mean you fell in a pit?"

"Yep."

Kate would've laughed if she wasn't trapped in an underground cave with the last person she wanted to be trapped in an underground cave with. Still, she was glad that she wasn't the only one who had fallen for Jersey and Ed's covered pit trick.

But that didn't actually explain why Ace was here in the first place. "What are you doing out here and why are you digging up the cave?" Kate gestured to where he had been chiseling away the stone.

Ace glanced back over his shoulder. "Let's just say the FBI has a vested interest in Itizuma's tomb."

Kate scrunched her face up. "Really? Since when does the FBI care about archaeological finds?"

Ace sighed. "I told you before this is more than just an archaeological find."

Kate walked over to the stone, surprised to find that it contained the winged frogs similar to those she'd found on the skull. They were leaping away in what looked like a path similar to the one on the skull. She didn't know how Ace had gotten his information that led him to this part of Mexico, but he might know more than she did about these leaping frogs. Kate realized the frogs could very well be the final piece of the map that she needed to locate the tomb.

Why would Ace be here by himself looking for the tomb? And why had he been in the market earlier when the hookah man had been murdered?

She whirled around to face him. "Are you sure you came with the FBI? Where are your partners?"

Ace's face crumbled and Kate felt a stab of regret. His cheek ticked as he answered her question. "The FBI is interested in the tomb. Like I said, this goes way beyond any kind of monetary or historical find. But I can't lie to you. I *did* come out early without my partners."

"Why?"

Ace sighed. "So that I could find you." He took a step closer and put his hands on her shoulders, pulling her toward him so close that she had to tilt her head back to look up at his face. "I could never forgive myself if anything happened to you."

Ace's lips slowly made their way toward Kate's, causing her heart to constrict in a battle of emotions. She wasn't sure whether she wanted to collapse in his arms or push them away and run in the other direction. Running was probably best, but much to her dismay, her traitorous body stayed frozen on the spot, her lips puckering, her eyes closed in anticipation …

"Hey, is someone down there?"

Their lips only millimeters apart, Kate and Ace jerked their heads in the direction of the voice coming from the top of the pit. Kate pushed Ace away and ran for the light.

"Heellooo!" the voice called and Kate recognized it as belonging to Ed.

Ace appeared at her side. "Who's that?"

"It's Jersey's assistant, Ed," she whispered.

"The archaeologist?" Ace asked. "Can we trust him?"

Kate wondered how much Ace knew about Jersey. Everything had happened so fast in the cave that she hadn't even had a chance to tell him about her run-in with Snake Ring and Jersey's betrayal.

Kate didn't know if they could trust Ed. She'd certainly thought he was not to be trusted before, but that was when she thought he was pulling one over on Jersey. Now that she knew Jersey was the one not to be trusted did that mean that Ed was a good guy?

Either way, the ladder was their only way out. She cupped her hands over her mouth and yelled, "We're down here!"

Ed's face appeared over the edge of the pit. "Kate! I heard what happened with Jersey. I'll lower the ladder. I have something for you."

Alarm bells went off in Kate's head. Why was Ed acting friendly all of a sudden? Could it be a trap? She glanced at Ace and could see he was having the same feelings of mistrust. But they needed the ladder and she *was* curious about what Ed had.

"Wait," Ace said. "I think we need the stone. I think it's part of a map to the tomb."

They started back into the cave and Kate whipped out her cell phone. "We don't need the stone, I'll just take a picture."

"Good idea." Ace's brows pinched together. "Why didn't I think of that?"

Kate tried to hide the smug smile that appeared on her face while she snapped the pictures. "So, what makes you think this is a map anyway?"

"I know a lot more about this than you think," Ace whispered while they walked back toward the pit opening. "We've been researching this back at the bureau and we know there are ancient codes or hieroglyphs that make up this map. It seems to be split up among various items, though, and we don't have them all."

Kate looked at the pictures on her phone. They were similar to the ones in the skull. Then she tapped her watch and looked at the pictures of what Gideon had found under the painting. She hadn't looked at it earlier. She'd been too astonished to see the picture of Ed with Reginald White. But now she could see that if she lined the two pictures up, they did almost look like some kind of map or path to something.

She looked closer at the images from the skull and it almost looked like a pyramid at the end of the path of frogs. Could that be the tomb? But *how* did one get to that path?

As she flipped quickly through the pictures, she could see that the images from the rock looked like they fit in between the images and the ones from the painting as if each one was a continuation of the same map. Maybe this was some sort of path they could follow, but she still didn't have a starting point. She wondered if Ace had that piece.

She narrowed her eyes at him. "So, what other pieces of this map do you have?"

"Just what was under that half of the painting." Ace looked at her out of the corner of her his eyes. "By the way, I know that was you in the *Lowenstaff Museum*."

"Where are you?" Ed's voice called down from the top of the pit, and Kate shut her phone off and stuffed it in her pocket as they made their way back out to the opening.

Ed lowered the ladder and Kate's taste of freedom was spoiled by thoughts of what Ed might have in store for them when they got to the top. Then again, if he wanted them out of the way, why not leave them down in the pit?

Ace gestured toward the ladder. "After you."

Kate shrugged and climbed up, her walking stick at the ready, just in case. But her fears were unfounded. When she got to the top, Ed did nothing more than give her a helping hand. Even so, she had to admit she felt a flutter of relief when Ace emerged from the pit and the three of them were standing at the top.

"How did you know we would be down there?" Kate half expected Ed to whip out a gun and point it at her, but all he had in his hand was a beat-up old leather journal.

"I saw what happened at the campsite. I came out of the forest to find a dead guy and Jersey causing the avalanche in the cave. I fought with Jersey and she got away, then I tried to dig out the rocks, but you didn't answer when I yelled in. I thought you were dead or had found a way out so I tried to chase Jersey because I think she knows where the tomb is. And I saw someone had fallen in the pit. Figured maybe you'd found your way out of the cave and then fell in again."

Ace slid questioning eyes over to Kate. "Again?"

Kate bristled. "That's not important now and *I* did not fall in, but I guess it doesn't matter. What does matter is how you know about the tomb. I thought you were excavating a Mayan village. You never said anything about a tomb." An edge of suspicion crept into Kate's voice.

She was shocked when Ed actually blushed. "I guess you found me out. I'm not actually who I pretended to be."

"Who are you?" Kate fisted her hands on her hips and looked between Ed and Ace. "Are you FBI, too?"

"No." They said at the same time.

"Well, then who are you with and why are you pretending to be an assistant sent by Jersey's bosses?"

"Look, we don't have time for that now." Ed brushed off her questions. "After Jersey ran off, I found this journal in her tent. She's obsessed with finding the tomb and I think once you look in here you'll see why. She's dangerous and it seemed like she got some clue as to where the tomb is."

Kate remembered Snake Ring's paper that Jersey had torn out of her hands and wondered if it was the missing piece of the map. Had Jersey already acquired the other pieces?

"Anyway," Ed continued. "She was heading toward your campsite and I'm afraid your people may be in trouble."

"How do you know where my site is?" Kate's mind

flashed back to all the times she'd felt like someone had been following her in the jungle. Had it actually been Ed? She glanced over at Ace. Or maybe it had been Ace? Then again, how did Snake Ring find her at Jersey's site if he hadn't been following her? For all she knew, all three of them had been following her.

"I make it my business to know what is going on." Ed shoved the book into her hand. "Read this, it will explain a lot."

Kate took the journal. It was soft, worn from decades of use. She untied the leather cord that wrapped around it. The cover flipped open, revealing papers that were yellowed and stained. The light blue fountain pen ink was barely visible. The front page had one sentence on it.

This is the journal of Reginald White.

"Reginald White?" Kate looked up at Ed in confusion. "The archaeologist?"

Ed nodded. "Reginald White was Jersey's grandfather. She's obsessed with carrying on his work."

Maybe that explained why the picture Gideon had sent of Reginald White showed a man who looked exactly like Ed. "Did one of your relatives have an association with Reginald White?"

"Sort of," he stammered. "There's no time to get into that now. Jersey has reached a boiling point. She's dangerous and we need to stop her."

Kate still wasn't sure if she trusted Ed, but Ace must've already made up his mind.

"Well, then let's go," Ace said. "Where is she?"

"That's the problem. I don't know exactly where she is. She was holding a piece of paper. It sounded like she said something about the last piece of the puzzle and then she took off. I would have followed her but I thought Kate needed my help," Ed said apologetically.

Kate was only half paying attention. She was busy flipping through the pages of the journal, which appeared to be an account of Reginald White's archaeological dig done in this area some thirty years ago. A series of flying winged frogs on a page at the end caught her eye—the same kind of frogs that were on the skull, the rock, and the archway they'd found earlier that morning.

She thought about the map. So far, she only had three of the pieces—the piece on the skull, the piece on the rock Ace had been digging, and the piece that Gideon had found under the painting. But none of these were the beginning pieces. It was possible that piece was on the other half of the painting which Jersey now had.

But if so, what was this in the book? She turned the book over and looked at it from the opposite side her breath catching in her throat when she recognized something on it. At the very end of the line of frogs was the symbol, the tattoo she'd seen on the hookah man and on Ed—the figure eight snake. That wasn't the main thing that had caught Kate's eye—*that* thing made her realize this was probably the missing piece to the puzzle. The beginning of the map that would lead to the tomb.

"I think I know how to find the tomb!"

———

Kate got out her compass app and spun around, looking for magnetic north. She looked at Ed. "You seem to know this place pretty good. Which direction is my camp."

"That way." Ed pointed toward the east. "You guys go ahead. I'll be right behind you. It's better not to go in together. That way we'll have the element of surprise."

"Let's go." Kate started off in a sprint. It was hard going, though, and they eventually had to slow down, picking their way through the thin paths that traversed the jungle. Kate's fingers brushed the soft leather book in her pocket and she wondered if it was the real deal or something Ed was using to throw them off track. She wouldn't put it past him, but she didn't really have anything better to go on and getting to her campsite and making sure her parents and the *Golden Capers* gang were okay wasn't a bad idea. Besides, he'd just pulled them out of the pit—why would he do that and then send them on a wild goose chase with a fake journal?

Ace came up beside her. "What was Ed talking about back there? Did Jersey kill Maxon and trap you in the cave?"

"Maxon?"

"Burgess Maxon, Markovic's guy that you were chasing in the market."

"Oh, right. I'd forgotten his name. She did kill him. I didn't have time to bring you up to speed in the cave." Kate filled Ace in on what had happened that morning. Glancing behind her to make sure Ed wasn't there, she leaned in toward Ace and whispered, "And the strangest part is Gideon showed me a picture of Reginald White and he was with a man who looked exactly like Ed."

"That's why you asked if his grandfather worked with Reginald."

Kate nodded. "He must have. But the other weird thing is that Ed and the man who was killed in the market have the exact same tattoo … and that tattoo is also right here in Reginald's book."

Ace frowned. "Really? That seems like a strange coincidence. What is the tattoo of?"

Kate shivered. "It's awful. It's a snake in a figure eight, eating its own tail."

Ace stopped in his tracks. "A figure eight? Let me see."

Kate flipped open the book carefully to the page pointing at the symbol. "This is it right here."

Ace's brows shot up. He turned the book to the side, angling it so that Kate could see the snake sideways instead of a figure eight. "Kate, that's not a figure eight. That's the infinity sign. That proves the FBI's theory about Itizuma."

Kate slapped her arms against her side, grabbing the book back from him. "What is this theory? You've been very elusive about it so far and I'd appreciate it if you'd just tell me what it is."

He shrugged. "Okay, but you may not believe me. This infinity symbol symbolizes much more than just forever. It's also a symbol for time travel."

Kate scrunched up her face. "Time travel? I thought that was just something that happened in science fiction. And you expect me to believe this Itizuma guy knew the secrets of time travel six hundred years ago?"

Ace's face turned grim. "That's exactly what I'm telling you. In the tomb is a codex that has the formula for time travel. That's why the FBI is interested. If this formula got in the wrong hands, it could be disastrous. Governments could use it to go back in time and change the outcome of wars. Can you imagine what that would do?"

Kate felt like she'd swallowed a boulder. She hadn't really thought of time travel before but when Ace put it that way, it seemed like it could be pretty bad. What if the Allies had not won World War II? Or George Washington had been assassinated? Kate shuddered to think what the world would be like today if ill-meaning people could go back in time and change things.

She felt silly. The whole time she was thinking she was digging up a tomb filled with riches and it was really much more than that. No wonder Jersey was so hot to get at it.

"Reginald White must have known about that." Kate shut the book and tapped the cover. "And judging by this map, it looks like he might have found the tomb. Jersey probably knew, too. She knew what was in that tomb was much more valuable than gold. She could use it for her own purposes or sell it to terrorists or an enemy government."

"That's right," Ace said. "And I'm afraid it's up to us to stop her."

CHAPTER
TWENTY-THREE

Kate eventually recognized the path that led to the archway they had found earlier that morning. When they got to the clearing, her stomach sank. It was empty. Where were her parents?

Kate flipped the book open to the map she'd seen earlier. Reginald's drawing looked like the archway or how it would have looked had it not fallen down.

"Look right here." She tapped on the archway in the book. "I think that is this." She pointed to the two broken columns and then took Ace over to where the remainder of the archway lay.

She pointed to what would have been the top of the arch. "If you put it back together, it would look similar to the archway in the book."

Ace pressed his lips together. "Yes, it does. So, you think this is the beginning of the map?"

"Yes. And if we follow the path, then we just need to put the middle pieces from the painting and the rock together with the end piece from the skull and it should lead us to the tomb."

"Great. But how do we decipher these."

Kate stared at the images. They were just frogs leaping off in different directions. But, as she looked at them, she realized the frogs were each a little different. Their wings were set at different angles. The angles reminded her of a compass.

"That's it!" These frogs correlate to compass points. If you look at these three frogs with their wings in this position, it's three frogs north and then this next frog points east. See what I mean?" She looked hopefully at Ace.

"Yes, I do. Too bad we don't know what unit of measurement a frog is. Is that a foot … a mile?"

Kate's spirits sank. "You're right. We won't know how far to go in each direction."

"Wait a minute. Let me see one of the maps."

Kate didn't want to open the leather book which sat safely in her pocket. It was too fragile and she was afraid the pages would fall apart. She pulled out her cell phone and brought up one of the pictures she had taken in the cave.

Ace took the phone from her and used his forefinger and thumb to enlarge the picture then he held it up to her. "Look at this right here." He tapped a spot in between two of the frogs. "This looks like something on the map almost as if they put signposts or markers where you were supposed to change direction. See how this frog is going north and the next one goes east."

"So there might be some kind of a sign, like maybe a tablet or a stone that will tell us when we need to change direction?" Kate asked.

Ace shrugged. "We might as well try it. We've got nothing else to go on. Your friend Ed hasn't shown up and besides, we don't even know if he can help."

Hope fluttered in Kate's chest. As she looked more closely at the maps, she saw there were small marks at every direction change. What Ace suggested made perfect sense. "The markers might not still be there after all this time, but I'm game if you are."

They started at the remains of the archway, just like the map in Reginald White's book indicated. Following the direction of the frogs, they walked north using the compass to make sure they were going in a straight line. Ace kept them on track while Kate scoured the ground for some sort of mark.

She was almost out of hope when she saw it. A four-inch tall piece of white, rectangular limestone stuck out of the ground. Its top was carved in a point, like a miniature pyramid.

"Over here! This can't be natural. Someone put this here on purpose."

Further inspection of the stone yielded a figure eight snake symbol. Kate and Ace smiled at each other. She was confident now that they were on the right path.

They continued following the map through the dense tropical forest, Kate's stomach getting tighter and tighter the further they traveled. She hadn't seen any sign of her parents and the *Golden Capers* gang. What had

Jersey done with them?

They never saw Ed, either, which only added to her stress. Once again, she considered the possibility that Ed had given them the book to throw them off track. But if he had, why did it all makes so much sense? And why did the map seem to be working out perfectly? Although they hadn't figured out what unit of measure each frog symbolized, they had noticed that the more frogs were piled up in each direction, the longer it took before they found a signpost. Clearly the frogs had some meaning, but it was beyond Kate to figure what it was.

After the first half hour, the jungle got thicker, making it harder to find the signposts. Kate became more and more frustrated. Would they ever get to the tomb? And what would they find when they got there?

"Shhh." Ace held out his arm for her to stop. "Do you hear that?"

Was someone following them? Maybe it was Ed. Kate strained to listen but didn't hear anything except the sounds of the forest. "I don't hear anyone."

"Not anyone, anything." Ace gestured for her to give him the phone and she did. He navigated to the picture of the skull, enlarging it and then holding it up for her to look at. "See these lines over here? I think that indicates a river and I hear one just to the east of us."

Kate cocked her ear in that direction. He was right. she heard the unmistakable sound of flowing water. She hadn't noticed it earlier because it didn't seem out of place, blending into the forest sounds naturally.

"If this map is correct, the tomb is at the mouth of this river. We just need to follow the river and I think we'll find it. And luck must be on our side because the sound of the river will mask our approach and will give us the element of surprise."

CHAPTER TWENTY-FOUR

Centuries of water rushing through the ancient river had cut a chasm in the ground. They followed alongside it as the map indicated, the chasm growing deeper as they progressed. Kate's stomach swooped every time she looked down.

Kate was glad she had brought her walking stick. It had scared off a few snakes along the way and the frequency of snake sightings seemed to increase the further they went.

"We must be getting close." Their journey had progressed through the various maps and they were now on the last one, which Kate assumed ended at the tomb. Judging from how far they thought they'd progressed in relation to the map, they should be coming up on it soon. Kate just hoped they'd be able to see it in the dense foliage.

She needn't have worried. They river took a sharp turn and there it was.

"Holy moly. I guess that's it, huh?" Ace said.

"Yes. It looks like this old map was pretty accurate after all." Kate stared at the step pyramid which rose up out of the forest. It wasn't the whole pyramid, though. Like most of these ancient ruins, one side had crumbled and fallen. They weren't close enough to see it, but Kate pictured the stone would be strewn about at the base, covered in moss and dirt. The top was just a jagged outline of what it once had been. Halfway up was a platform similar to that which usually sat on top of these types of pyramids and would typically be used as a temple.

On that platform, Kate could see Jersey, Kate's parents and the *Golden Capers* gang.

Panic lapped at Kate's gut. It looked like Jersey had them as hostages and was threatening them with something. She didn't know what Jersey was doing, but whatever it was, it didn't look good for the *Golden Capers* gang. "What's going on up there?"

"I don't know. Let's sneak up a little closer and find out," Ace whispered. "We don't want her to know we're here."

They wove their way through the thick foliage, being careful not to make any sound or movement that might alert Jersey to their presence. Kate could see that the pyramid backed up against the edge of the river. The side of the temple that backed up to the river had deteriorated and sheered off steeply. The platform where her parents stood dropped off sharply, straight to the edge of the cliff. It must have been a one hundred foot fall and it looked like Jersey was aiming to push them off.

Kate's heart crowded her throat as she watched Jersey advance toward the huddled group that made up her parents and close friends. They took a backward step. There were mere inches now between them and the edge of the platform.

Kate could see they were tied together somehow, ankle to ankle, their wrists bound behind them. One false move by one of them and they'd all topple, pulling each other over the side. Had Jersey managed to do that on her own? She must have had help, but where was that help now? It looked like Jersey was the only bad guy up there.

"They'll fall to their deaths!" Kate started to run toward the pyramid but Ace pulled her back.

"You can't just rush in there like that or she probably will push them off," he whispered in her ear.

Of course, he was right. She couldn't just go off half-cocked and rush Jersey with only a walking stick for a weapon. What had she been thinking? She needed a better plan. And then one came to her. She turned to Ace.

"You're right. Can you shoot her from here without hitting anyone else?" Kate hunkered down behind a large-leafed plant, her eyes glued to Jersey, anticipating the kill shot that would send the blonde archaeologist tumbling down the pyramid's steep steps.

No shot came.

She looked back over her shoulder at Ace. "What are you waiting for? Can't you get a clean shot?"

Ace hesitated. "It's not that … I don't have a gun."

Kate's brows pinched together. She whirled around

to look at him. "What? What kind of FBI agent goes out without a gun? Are you joking?"

She looked up and down and then wondered where she thought he would have hidden a gun. His gray, sweat-covered T-shirt clung tightly to his nicely formed chest and tapered waist. There was no bulge for a gun. Where had she thought he would keep it? In the pocket of his cargo shorts?

Ace ran his hand through his short-cropped hair. His face turned sheepish. "Well, I'm not actually out here with the bureau."

"I knew it," she hissed. "You're with the bad guys."

Ace held up his hands. "No. Nothing like that. I might have exaggerated before when I implied I came out *ahead* of my partners. The truth is they don't even know I'm out here. Oh, they planned to send us, but they were taking so long and you were here in danger … I came out to make sure you didn't get hurt and figured if I did a little recon about the tomb, it would help when my team finally did get here. But since I wasn't on official business, I left my gun at home. The gun is only for official FBI business, you know."

Kate rolled her eyes. Leave it to by-the-book Ace Mason to leave his gun at home.

"Don't you have a gun in one of your pockets?" Ace indicated Kate's multi-purpose vest.

"No." Kate could smack herself. Why hadn't she thought to bring a gun? She wasn't used to carrying one and everything had happened so fast, she didn't even think to get it when she was back at the camp.

Snatches of the conversation going on up on the platform drifted down to them. She couldn't make out the actual words,, only that Gertie was saying something sarcastic and Jersey was saying something threatening. She looked up and saw Jersey poke her stick at Gertie, who shuffled backward, the heel of her shoe heart-stoppingly close to the edge of the platform.

If they waited any longer, her parents and the *Golden Capers* gang—the only family she'd ever known—would plunge to their deaths in the river below. She couldn't let that happen.

"I'm going in!" She pushed Ace away and sprinted toward the temple.

———

Kate was vaguely aware of Ace yelling for her to come back, but his words were drowned out by her thudding heartbeat as she sprinted for the pyramid. Reaching the steps, she took them two at a time, her only weapon the walking stick held out in front of her.

Jersey heard her coming and turned to face her, holding the long, pointy weapon at her to stop her advance. Now that Kate was closer, she could see it was some sort of hook spear with a long, pointy blade. Jersey swished it through the air like a Kung Fu master. It looked menacing, but Kate was more relieved that Jersey wasn't pointing it at her parents than concerned about her own welfare.

She pressed the button on the handle of her walking stick and the knife slid out. She'd have to fight Jersey on her own terms.

Kate surged up the last of the steps, confident that she could beat the blonde archaeologist. But when she got to the top, she skidded to a stop, the confidence draining out of her.

The platform where Jersey and the *Golden Capers* gang stood was not one solid surface like she had thought. It was broken up into different areas-the solid surface at the top of the steps where Kate stood and another solid surface at the back of the temple platform that backed up to the cliff leading to the river. Those surfaces were no problem. What *was* the problem was what was in between—two giant pits too wide for Kate to jump across.

The pits weren't really the problem, either. The problem was they were both filled with angry, writhing snakes.

Kate froze in her tracks. She stared down at the mass of wriggling, slimy bodies. She could see all different kinds of snakes. Some were all black, some brown and tan with a pattern, some solid brown with stripes. Were any of them poisonous?

Her stomach turned inside out, her vision started to fade and her knees grew weak as the hissing of the snakes filled her ears.

"You can do it, Kate!" Her mother's voice pulled her attention from the writhing reptiles and tugged her back from the brink of unconsciousness.

She looked over to see the smug look on Jersey's face.

"What's the matter? You don't like snakes?" Jersey taunted her. "Well, that's too bad. I was hoping to push you off the cliff with your parents but if you die in the pit of snakes it's all the same to me. Either way, I get to discover the tomb and I will be the owner of the riches and the most important item—Itizuma's codex."

Kate frowned. Did Jersey think the tomb was inside this pyramid? Maybe Jersey didn't know that most Aztec pyramids were solid dirt. Boy, was she gonna be mad when she found out there was no tomb in the pyramid. Kate felt a little let down herself—had the map been just a ruse? Or was there really a secret tomb at another location nearby? At the realization of Jersey's mistake, some of Kate's bravado returned.

"I think you might be disappointed," Kate said. "The tomb isn't in here."

Jersey snickered. "Of course it is. Gramps wrote about it in his journal and Burgess Maxon provided me with the last piece of the map that I needed and I followed it here. Too bad these old people got in my way. But that's okay. I don't mind killing all of you."

Jersey turned her attention back to the *Golden Capers* gang at the edge of the platform and Kate felt a jolt of panic.

"Wait! You're doing this all for nothing. Your grandfather was wrong. There is no tomb!" Jersey stopped in her tracks, turning back to look at Kate in confusion. Kate realized she'd struck a nerve. She had Jersey off guard now and had to act quick.

Kate looked down at the snakes, who seemed to be hissing even louder. Their beady, gold, slitted eyes looking up at her sent a surge of terror through her veins.

But she couldn't fight Jersey from over here. She'd have to get to Jersey's side and the only way to do that was to jump across the pit.

Studying the area, Kate saw there were actually two pits with narrow walkways in between. She only had two choices. She could throw the walking stick—her only weapon—like a javelin and hope that it hit Jersey and injured her enough for her parents to escape. Or she could leap across the walkways to get to Jersey.

The javelin throw was a long shot. Jersey could easily dodge out of the way and Kate would be left with no weapon. So, the only thing to do was to jump onto the narrow walkway.

She looked down at the pit again and started to get that woozy feeling. Her limbs felt like they were mired in mud. Her mind was telling them to jump but they wouldn't move. It was a familiar sensation, the same sensation she'd felt in the steam tunnel and on that fateful day back in Stockholm.

"You can do it, Kate!" This came from behind her. It was Ace.

Where had he been?

His voice dragged her out of the frozen state. She looked up at Jersey's smirking face and then at the *Golden Capers* gang and she felt a surge of warmth and love chase away the frozen terror. These were her people and she *had* to save them.

Kate closed her eyes and jumped.

———

Kate braced herself for the slimy, rubbery feeling of snakes crawling on her. But she didn't feel that—instead, her feet met solid ground. Her eyes flew open. She'd managed to make it to one of the walkways. It was only about a foot wide but wide enough for her to gain her purchase.

The snakes hissed louder, as if to show their disappointment that she hadn't fallen into the pit.

Across the second snake pit, Jersey's eyes widened. She seemed to be completely astonished that Kate had jumped over the snakes, which made Kate wonder how Jersey had gotten the *Golden Capers* gang up there in the first place. Was there another way up onto the platform? There must have been, but that wouldn't do her any good now as she was straddled between the two pits. She'd need to jump across the second one in order to do battle with Jersey. A second way down *would* come in handy, though, once she'd defeated the antagonistic archaeologist.

Kate glanced down at the snakes again but this time they didn't bother her nearly as much. She'd already jumped over one pit.

She could do this.

On the other side, Jersey was at the ready with her stick, which Kate saw was pointy and red on the end. Had she already stabbed somebody with it? Kate didn't want to think about that. She balanced her walking stick in both hands and jumped over the second snake pit, landing directly in front of a surprised Jersey.

Faced with an opponent who had a foil-like weapon,

Kate's training quickly came back to her and she instinctively moved into a fencing stance.

"On guard!" She couldn't believe she'd actually said that.

Jersey snickered and jabbed at Kate's chest. Kate deftly moved out of the way, swishing her walking stick toward Jersey's face.

Jersey stumbled back and Kate jabbed toward her middle. But Jersey was quick. She spun out of the way and managed to land a blow on Kate's shoulder.

Kate fumbled the walking stick. She recovered it at the last minute, but not before Jersey landed another blow on her ankle, causing her to stumble and almost fall into the snake pit. She spun away quickly, jabbing out in Jersey's direction and connecting with her arm. Satisfaction flooded through her when she saw a flash of blood well up on Jersey's bicep. Too bad it wasn't enough of a wound to stop her from coming forward.

Kate was vaguely aware of her parents and the *Golden Capers* gang cheering her on. Remembering her fencing training, she blocked out all outside influences and focused on the moves—slashing right and then left, then spinning to avoid Jersey's clumsy jabs.

"Kate! Look out!" Ace's voice came from behind her. She glanced over quickly to see that he'd come up to the edge of the first snake pit with a long tree branch which was sharpened at the end. She'd wondered what he'd been doing all this time. Apparently, he'd been fashioning himself a weapon.

But the momentary distraction cost her. Jersey lunged forward, ramming her stick into Kate's side.

Kate doubled over, falling hard onto the stone platform.

Jersey loomed over her, holding the stick high over her head to administer the fatal blow. But the blonde archaeologist's triumphant cry had the opposite effect on Kate. Instead of making her give up, it gave her a surge of energy. Kate catapulted up from her position on the ground with the knife end of the walking stick thrust out toward Jersey's torso.

The blade made a sickening squishy sound as it penetrated Jersey's rib cage.

Jersey's eyes widened and then darkened with anger. Kate could see the red stain on her shirt. She'd done some good damage but Jersey was still on her feet. Kate's side started to throb.

"You won't win!" Jersey threw down the stick and launched herself at Kate, who stood with her heels at the very edge of the snake pit.

Kate teetered backward, her arms grabbing at thin air in a futile attempt to pull herself back onto the platform. She tried to lean forward, but gravity was stronger and the momentum kept her falling back. She felt her feet leave the platform and shot a panicked glance over her shoulder, just in time to see dozens of golden, slitted snake eyes rushing toward her.

CHAPTER TWENTY-FIVE

Kate's hip exploded in pain as she hit the stone slab. Contrary to what she'd expected, she did not land in a rubbery pile of snakes. The snakes had all slithered out of the way when she'd fallen. Maybe they didn't want to get crushed and ruin the opportunity to eat her.

The panic that had welled up in her chest paralyzed her and she lay there for a few seconds

"Kate!" Ace's voice drifted down from above. She looked up in time to see him leaping into the pit. He landed with a thud beside her.

She whipped her head around to get a bead on the location of the snakes and look for some way to get out of the pit before they attacked her. She noticed something strange—the snakes were making a bee-line out of the pit, slithering off through narrow slits on the side of the platform. Now why would they do that? Unless, somehow, they knew it was dangerous to stay in the pit.

Before she could voice a warning to Ace, the platform gave a sickening lurch, pivoting at a ninety-degree angle. Kate slid down the length of it, her nails scraping the smooth stone as she tried to stay on top. Despite her efforts, she kept sliding into the darkened maw of the bowels of the pyramid.

"What the…" Ace echoed her thoughts as she thudded onto something hard, landing on the same hip and causing even more pain.

The stone slab sprang shut just as quickly as it had dumped them and they were in complete darkness. They sat, unmoving for a few seconds while their eyes adjusted to the darkness. Kate mentally scanned her body for broken bones, but everything felt fine. Even the pain in her hip was receding.

She smelled herbs and old dirt and water. She could hear water running somewhere. She didn't know how far they'd fallen, but they must be close to the level of the river.

"Did what I think just happened just happen?" Ace asked.

"You mean did we just fall into a pit of snakes and then get dumped into the inside of a temple which shouldn't even be hollow?" Kate squinted her eyes. She was starting to be able to see shadows. This definitely was not an empty room.

Looking around, she could see the space was cavernous and the floor wasn't dirt—it had hurt too much when she'd landed on it—it was something harder. As her eyes adjusted, the shadows took the form of statues, pillars and murals around the room. In the middle sat a large, rectangular object. Her heart skipped a beat.

Was it possible that they were inside Itizuma's tomb?

"I have a flashlight on my phone." Kate scrambled for her phone, hoping it hadn't been jarred out of her pocket in the fall. She found it, pressed the flashlight app and aimed it into the room, tentatively hoping it didn't illuminate more snakes.

It didn't. What it did illuminate sucked the breath right out of her.

The room was constructed of large, polished limestone blocks. Carvings and hieroglyphs decorated the walls. Large statues were placed along the walls, some of them covered in turquoise tiles. A niche carved out of the wall held dozens of zoomorphic figures in gold and jade.

And in the center, just as she'd suspected, was a sarcophagus. It was not unlike that of an Egyptian sarcophagus, Kate realized, as she played her light over it. Shaped like a rectangle, the top was carved to resemble a human body. Except instead of the Egyptian humanlike form, this was more geometric, much like the Aztecs' carvings on the walls.

"Wow. There must be a fortune in gold and gemstones in here." Ace walked around the perimeter of the room, looking at the various carvings, sculptures and trinkets.

He stopped in front of a large niche with what looked

like a thick piece of paper.

"So, it really is true." His voice was barely above a whisper.

Kate joined him. She could see the piece of paper had been preserved pretty well over the centuries. She guessed the absence of airflow in the tomb had helped.

"Is that the codex?"

"Yes. It's on fig bark, all handwritten in hieroglyphs."

"What does it say?" Kate asked

"I have no idea. An expert would have to translate it, but if what I'm told is true, this contains the secret to time travel."

Kate stared at it for a while, trying to make sense of the symbols. Something on the floor caught her eye.

"What's this?" Kate pointed to a small piece of paper on the floor in front of the niche. This paper was not fig bark. It was more modern but still decades old. It was yellowed with age and contained light blue fountain pen, much like that in the journal.

Ace picked it up, his eyes growing wide as he read it. "I think this is from Reginald White."

Kate looked over his shoulder at the paper. It was just a small scrap, but on it was written, 'I have discovered the secret. Will test the time. See you on the other side' and it was signed R.W.

Kate felt a bubble of excitement. "You mean Reginald White actually found this tomb?"

"Well, it looks like someone did. This paper isn't from Itizuma's time."

"But why didn't he make the discovery public? Cash in on it?" Kate asked.

Ace rubbed his hand over his chin, scruffy with a day's worth of growth. "Reginald White disappeared, or so everyone thought. They suspected foul play, but maybe he didn't actually disappear. Maybe he really did figure out how to time travel. No one ever found his body. Maybe he traveled through time and didn't want to come back."

"Or couldn't figure out *how* to come back," Kate added.

"Maybe." Ace grabbed Kate's shoulders, his face a mask of seriousness. "You realize what we've stumbled onto? If this really is the secret to time travel, we can't let anyone know it exists."

Kate's brows tugged. "Why not? It seems like this would be very important. A lot of people would want to know about this."

"Exactly. And what do you think those people would do with it? Sure, it could be useful for some things, but in my experience, most people would want to use it for something bad. Imagine how it would be if someone could go back in time and change the outcome of wars? What if they could kill off key political or religious figures before they became known? Governments would kill for this and they could totally change the course of history. No one can be trusted with this information ... not even our own government."

"Are you suggesting we simply not tell anyone? I think too many people already know about it." Kate said.

"There might be another solution." Ace scouted the perimeter of the room, looking in the various niches and muttering to himself. Finally, he nodded and turned to

Kate. "Do you hear the water?"

"Yes. I figured we're probably low in the pyramid, maybe even under the ground. Close to the river."

"Sort of. I think this pyramid is constructed with flood chambers. The water is running through them inside the pyramid."

"Flood chambers?" Kate asked. "You mean that you can somehow flood the tomb?"

"Yes," Ace said. "It was a common tactic that pirates used to use when they buried treasure. Maybe the pirates even learned it from the Aztecs." Ace shrugged. "Who knows? I'm pretty sure that removing these stones will cause the chamber to be flooded."

Kate thought about what that would mean. Max was counting on her to find the tomb, but did he know about the time travel codex? Kate figured he probably didn't.

She didn't know Max that well, but from what she knew of him, he wasn't a money-grubbing scientist. He just wanted good exhibits for the museum. If he knew this tomb contained the secret to time travel, he might not want it to be known, either.

She hated to go back to the museum empty-handed, but the evil ramifications of making time travel known to the world weren't lost on her. The responsibility weighed heavily.

She looked around the chamber at the gold, the jade, the turquoise and the amazing wealth of history and riches it contained. If they flooded the chamber, all of it would be lost forever. And so would the time travel codex.

"What if we just destroyed the codex?" she asked.

"I thought about that. But there's no way to know if there are other clues inside this chamber. There probably are. If you had that sort of information, would you trust it to a flimsy piece of fig bark?"

"I guess not." Kate's heart sank. Ace was right. The only way to be sure this information didn't get into evil hands was to flood the tomb. "Flooding the room seems like the right thing to do. How do we get out of here?" Kate asked.

The look on Ace's face made her heart twist. "That may be a problem. Near as I can tell, these flood stones open up the chambers that will send the water in, but if you look over here," Ace pointed to another stone that was at a ninety-degree angle from the flood stones, "it looks like this stone might open another passage."

Kate didn't understand why he had such a grave look on his face. "Okay, so we start flooding the chamber, go out the secret passage and shut the door on the other side. Easy peasy."

Ace grabbed her hand and pulled her over to him. She didn't like the look on his face at all. What was wrong with her plan?

"It's not that simple," he said. "Look at the position of the stones. You need to push the stone that opens the passageway to the chamber over to the left. But the flood stones need to be pushed to the right. Once the flood chambers are open, you can't open the passageway. And once the passageway is open you won't be able to activate the flood stones."

Kate stared at the stones. It looked like either you could exit the room, or you could flood it, but not both at the same time as the stones would be positioned in each other's way. "There's got to be another way out!"

Ace shook his head. "I went all around the room. You saw me. There's no other way. These are the only stones that activate anything."

"But that's impossible," Kate said. "You mean the chamber was designed to drown the person who floods it?"

"I'm afraid so. It kind of makes sense when you think about it, because it would be one way to ensure that the person flooding the chamber was serious about it."

"Deadly serious," Kate said. "Well, then, we can't flood it. We'll just have to lie about its discovery. We'll pretend we found nothing. We'll say it was empty."

Ace pulled her close. "You know that won't work. Someone is bound to find out and I'm afraid I can't let that happen." He tucked a lock of her hair behind her ear. "This is bigger than both of us. We *need* to flood this chamber, but I'm not going to let you die."

"What do you mean?" Kate's heart skittered around in her chest as she saw a flood of emotion pass through Ace's eyes.

"Kate. You've got to go. I'll open the door and you go out and activate the mechanism from the other side that closes the door, then I'll flood the chamber."

Kate's eyes darted from Ace's face to the stones. There had to be another way. Ace Mason had been a thorn in her side since he'd sacrifice her to the FBI, but for some reason, her heart was breaking at the thought of him not being around anymore.

"No! I won't let you die." The words tumbled from her lips.

Ace's face broke in a sad smile. "I knew you still cared about me. And that's why I can't let anything happen to you." He pushed the stone and the opening slid open. Beyond it was a dark corridor.

Kate's eyes ping-ponged between the opening and Ace.

"Go!" Ace demanded.

Emotions warred in Kate's chest. Her heart twisted at the thought of leaving Ace in there to die—would she ever be able to forgive herself? But her blood boiled at the high-handed way he'd ordered her to leave. She didn't take orders from anyone.

In a split second, she made her decision. She pushed him against the wall her lips seeking his. Her hand bumped against the stone that opened the passageway. The passageway silently slid closed—not that either of them was watching.

Ace pulled her closer, his lips burning against hers, causing her stomach to flip-flop. Her hand explored the wall behind her, feeling for the flood stone that jutted out two inches from the wall. She found it and then, with only a moment's hesitation, she pushed the stone to the left.

The sound of rocks scraping against rock filled the chamber, the flood channels opened and water rushed in.

CHAPTER TWENTY-SIX

Ace ripped his lips from hers and stared at the water swirling around their ankles incredulously. "What did you do?"

"I couldn't leave you to die alone." The water was freezing. Kate's feet were already getting numb. Maybe she'd been a bit too hasty in her decision.

"But now we'll both die."

Kate narrowed her eyes at Ace. He didn't sound very grateful for her sacrifice. He sounded mad. Probably pissed because she'd disobeyed his orders. Yep, that would be just like do-it-by-the-book Ace Mason. What had she been thinking?

She pushed herself away from him and pressed the stones frantically. "There has to be a way out."

Ace sighed. "I already told you, I looked over the wall pretty good. There isn't one."

"Well, we should look again. Unless you have something better to do?" Kate was shocked at how quickly the water was coming in. It was halfway to her knees and so cold it chilled the blood in her veins. She trudged to the opposite side of the room, her legs like wooden stubs. Her fingers explored the wall, pressing on anything that looked like it might open a trap door.

Ace was still over by the stones, grunting as he pushed on them to try to stop the water.

"Damn it!" He pounded on the wall.

Kate looked around the room frantically. Her eyes fell on the ceiling where they'd fallen into the tomb. She could see slits of light filtering in. The slits the snakes had gone through, apparently. But where were the snakes?

If the snakes had found a way out, maybe they could, too.

"What about up there?" She pointed to the ceiling.

Ace looked up. "The slits are too small to fit through. But maybe we can pull down the platform that we slid in on. It must have some sort of mechanism like a spring that caused it to dump us in here in the first place."

Kate felt a surge of hope. "How do we get up there?"

The ceiling was tall, maybe twenty feet above their heads And there was nothing to climb up on.

"I don't know," Ace shouted over the roaring water, which seemed to have gotten louder. It was coming in faster—the depth was now over her knees. "We could wait until the water floats us up but if our theory is wrong it won't be long until the chamber is full with no breathing area and we won't have a chance to look anywhere else."

Kate wrapped her arms around her shivering body. "Not to mention that we might succumb to hypothermia first."

Ace battled the current to get over to her. He pulled her into his arms. "I can't believe this is happening. I have to find a way to save you. I came all the way here to make sure nothing happened to you and now look what's happened. You're going to die because of me."

Kate's heart melted. Ace was almost in tears. She reached up and touched his face. His gray eyes were stormy with emotion.

He pulled her closer, his thumb stroking her cheek. "Kate, we may die in here and I'll never get the chance to tell you that I lo—"

His words were cut off by a loud squeal in the corner of the room. They whipped their heads around to see one of the statues moving. If Kate wasn't mistaken, it was swinging open as if it were a false door. She couldn't believe her eyes when a figure stepped out into the water.

"What the heck?" Ace released Kate and started toward the man. Kate was right on his heels.

The man was dressed in the most unusual outfit. He was wearing what looked like a long shirt that reached just below his crotch. The shirt was a colorful blue with gold designs. He wore no pants and he had a feather headdress on top of his head. And if Kate wasn't mistaken, he held a spear in his hand. Was he some sort of native that hadn't yet been introduced to Western clothes?

"Come. I will show you the way out." He gestured with his head to indicate the area inside the statue behind him which Kate saw was actually some sort of opening. The statue had been a fake and behind it were stairs leading up to a dark passage. She felt a tremor of trepidation. She didn't know if she could trust this guy—but, then again, staying in the rapidly filling chamber wasn't that appealing, either.

The man turned and walked up the steps. Kate shrugged at Ace and then followed him.

Kate climbed the narrow steps on numb feet, her hand trailing against the moist wall for balance. It took about twenty steps for her legs to start to thaw and in a few more steps they reached a landing that looked like some sort of intersection with tunnels going off in several directions. The man stopped in the middle.

"Who are you?" Kate asked.

"A friend," the man said simply.

Ace was a little less friendly. He stood with his feet shoulder width apart looking like he was spoiling for a fight.

"Who sent you? And why are you dressed like that?" Ace looked the man up and down.

Kate frowned at Ace. It was just like him to be so distrusting of a man who had just saved them from certain death … even if he was wearing what looked like a mini-dress. She was sure they taught that sort of antagonistic behavior in the FBI, though she didn't remember taking the class herself.

The man glanced down at himself, then leveled his brilliant blue eyes on Ace.

"We don't have time for these questions now. The pyramid is filling with water." He gestured back toward the stairs and Kate looked in that direction. She could hear the rushing water coming up the stairs and, judging by the rate the chamber had been filling up, it would reach them quickly.

Kate was glad they'd been saved from drowning in the chamber, but she didn't have time to sit around getting all sentimental about it. Since falling into the tomb, she'd been too busy to worry about her parents and the *Golden Capers* gang. Now that *she* was out of immediate danger, worry for her parents came flooding in. She didn't know if her blow had killed Jersey or not. For all she knew, her folks were at the bottom of the river.

"We don't have time for this. My parents are in danger! We need to get out of here now!" Kate's voice rose in panic.

"This is the way out." The man pointed toward the middle path. Kate's eyes followed the direction he was pointing and, catching a glance of his wrist, she gasped.

He had the infinity tattoo on his arm!

She looked up at him and saw he was watching her reaction. His eyes seemed to glow with a knowing light and he nodded at her. "You both must go quickly before the water finds us."

"But what about you?" Kate asked. It didn't seem like he was planning on going down the tunnel with them.

He pointed to another path and smiled. "Don't worry, I will be fine ... I will see you in another time."

Kate didn't have time to stick around and ask him what he meant by that strange remark. Her parents needed her. She sprinted off down the tunnel.

———

"You're going to just follow what that weird guy tells you to do?" Ace sprinted along behind her.

Kate hadn't really thought about it. For some reason she trusted the guy, but she supposed he could have been leading them into another snake den of danger. But if he wished them harm, why rescue them from the tomb?

"I don't see as we have much choice," she said.

"There were three passages we could have chosen. Any one of them could be the wrong one. We don't know if he was working with the bad guys to lead us into some danger!"

Kate frowned at Ace. "Well, sometimes you have to go with your gut. But you can feel free to go down any passage you want."

Ace made a snorting sound. "Going with your gut can get you into trouble."

"Right. You probably would have just shot him and we'd be heading down the wrong path now."

"I wouldn't have shot him," Ace argued. "I might have chosen the path a bit more thoughtfully, though. These rash decisions, like locking us both in the tomb and flooding it, can have disastrous consequences. If you'd followed my orders you'd be safe by now."

Kate's brows shot up. "And you'd be dead. Besides, we're not partners anymore and I don't have to follow your orders."

Kate sprinted faster, not sure if she was in more of a hurry to get *to* her parents or *away* from Ace. She remembered how impossible he could be and hoped she wouldn't regret not taking him up on his offer to get out of the tomb and leave him in there to drown.

Kate's breath came in short gasps. They were travel-
ing uphill and she was getting winded. Uphill was good,
though, because it meant they were heading away from
the water. But where would they end up? Would the tunnel lead to a dead end with an opening that plunged to
the river below?

A pinpoint of light up ahead told her she wouldn't
have to wait long to find out. She picked up speed.

The tunnel spilled out on the side of the pyramid.
She could see they were about three quarters of the way
up. Where were her parents?

Her stomach tightened as she strained to listen for
the sound of their voices, but all she could hear were the
birds calling in the forest.

"We need to get around to the front!" she said to Ace.

When she'd last seen her parents, they'd been on the
platform in the front of the pyramid and she figured this
was the best place to look now. The stone steps were very
narrow on this side but she didn't have time to go down
to the ground and then up the wider steps in the front, so
she shuffled along sideways to the edge of the pyramid,
peeking tentatively around the corner just in case Jersey
was lying in wait for her.

She angled her head to look up at the platform. It was
empty. She had visions of Jersey pushing her parents and
the *Golden Capers* gang off the back. She could almost
hear their screams as they plummeted toward the river.

"Kate!"

Wait a minute. Was that her mother?

Kate swiveled her head in the direction of the voice
which was coming from the bottom of the pyramid. Her

mouth hung open at what she saw. Vic, Carlotta, Sal, Gertie, Frankie and Benny were standing leisurely in the grass as if they were discussing the latest baseball scores. In between them, they had a large piece of paper which looked like a map.

"You escaped!" Kate was so excited, she lost her footing. She stumbled sideways, almost falling down the side of the pyramid until strong arms broke her fall.

"Whoa, there," Ace said.

Kate pushed his hands away.

"Thanks," she said brusquely.

She was still a little mad about his high-handed manner and the thought that she should take orders from him. Not to mention that whatever it was he had been trying to tell her before the strange man came out of the statue had made her a little nervous.

She needed time to think about her feelings for Ace, which had re-surfaced in the heat of the moment in the tomb. Until then, she didn't want to give him any false signals.

They both scurried down to the ground where Carlotta was waiting with open arms.

"We thought you guys were goners," Sal said.

"We thought the same of you," Kate admitted. "How did you get away? What happened to Jersey?"

Sal snickered, held up his hand and flipped out the blade on his prosthetic thumb. "While you and Jersey were having your sword fight, I was using my blade here to work on our ropes so we could get free."

"That jab that you gave to Jersey really hurt her. She didn't have much energy left after she pushed you into the snakes," Gertie said.

"Then that guy that was working with her … Ed? He came charging up the steps and the two of them got into it something fierce," Frankie added.

Benny nodded enthusiastically. "They got to fighting. One thing led to another and she fell off the edge into the river."

"Darn shame," Gertie tisked, then smiled, erasing any doubts as to whether she actually thought Jersey's fate really was a darn shame.

"We figured it was for the best." Carlotta shrugged. "But tell us what happened to you inside that pyramid. We feared the worst."

Kate and Ace exchanged a glance. Should they tell them about the tomb? Kate didn't think so. Even though she trusted her parents and the *Golden Capers* gang implicitly, it was probably better off for *them* if they didn't know about it. The less people to talk about the codex, the better.

"The inside of the pyramid is a big, empty room. I guess it must have been a temple for worship at one time, but everything's been looted." Kate slid her eyes over to look at Ace, who gave a tight nod.

"It had flood chambers from the river and when we got dumped in, a switch must have been flicked that started the flooding," Ace continued. "We were lucky enough to find some passages that led us out onto the other side of the pyramid."

They all looked up at the pyramid in time to see water running down the steps like a waterfall. The flooding must have reached the top. Kate remembered the little slits that the snakes had disappeared through. She figured the water was now pouring out of those and running down the steps.

It was for the best—no one would be able to get inside the tomb now. She belatedly wondered what happened to the snakes. Did they get away through the tunnels, or did they drown? She found herself hoping it was the latter. And what about the strange man they'd seen? Where was he now?

"We're just glad you got out. We were just about to go in after you," Benny tapped on the map. "This map shows the passages."

Kate frowned. "Where'd you get that?"

"That guy Ed gave it to us," Frankie said. "He said he found it in Jersey's things and thought we might need it. Somehow, he was worried you would get trapped inside. Don't know why he would think that, but apparently he was smarter than he looked."

Kate looked around the site. "Where *is* Ed, anyway?"

"It was the darnedest thing," Benny said. "He gave us the map and while we were bending over it and inspecting it the next thing we knew he was gone. Poof. Just like that."

Ace made a face. "What do you mean, *just like that*? The guy couldn't disappear. He must be around here somewhere."

Vic shrugged. "I don't know. One minute he was here and the next he was gone. To tell you the truth, I wasn't paying much attention. I was busy looking at the map and trying to figure out how to get Kate out."

"He must have just gone off into the woods," Ace suggested.

"Sure. That's probably what happened." Vic folded up the map. "Well, I guess we don't need this anymore."

"Yeah. It's too bad, though," Benny said. "We thought the tomb you were looking for might be in the pyramid."

"That's why we were here in the first place," Carlotta explained. "We'd been clearing out the area and following these little stone markers. When we saw this pyramid, we thought we hit pay dirt."

"We were all excited until Jersey showed up with those two helpers of hers and attacked us," Gertie said.

"I'm a bit embarrassed," Vic said. "But we weren't prepared and they took us pretty easy and tied us up."

"Yeah, plus she had a gun," Sal added. "Too bad we didn't find out it was out of bullets until she had forced us up onto the top platform."

"But how did you get up onto the platform anyway?" Kate asked. "How did you get past the snake pits?"

"Oh, there was another way to get up on the side, but after Jersey got us up there, she hit some weird stone that made it impassable. We had a heck of a time getting back down, but luckily that guy Ed knew just where to step."

Gertie waved her hand in the air. "That woman was completely bonkers. She even pushed her own helpers off the back after they helped her tie us up."

"We were almost killed." Sal's face crumpled. "And it was all for nothing."

"I had a run-in with Jersey myself." Kate explained what had happened with Jersey and Snake Ring, then how she'd gotten stuck in the cave, found Ace and discovered the rest of the maps. She pulled out her cell phone and showed them the pictures. "So we followed the maps to this pyramid. We had no idea Jersey had you trapped up here, though. We thought we would find the tomb."

"So then there really is no tomb?" Gertie's face fell in disappointment.

Kate spread her hands. "I guess not. The maps all lead to this temple, so it seems like it would be here if it was anywhere. Maybe it was here once but got looted over the years."

"Either that or it was just a legend. The Aztecs didn't really bury their rulers in big tombs like the Egyptians did, so it was kind of a long shot in the first place," Ace said.

"Wow," Vic said. "So, the museum spent all this money for us to come out here for nothing?"

"Yeah. I hope Max isn't going to be mad at you," Gertie added.

Kate felt a sinking sensation. She hoped Max wasn't going to be mad at her, too, but she had no intention of telling Max that they'd found the tomb and then flooded it.

She thought back to how she'd been stuck with all that desk work because of that little incident in Stockholm. A feeling of pride spread in her chest, she hadn't frozen when faced with the snakes at the top of the tomb. That was progress.

She didn't know if Max would see it that way, though. He might just see this as a failure to complete her mission. And if he did, would he stick her on a desk job again?

Kate glanced back up at the pyramid. It didn't really matter now. The tomb was under water and she knew in her heart that she'd done the right thing and that was more important than impressing her boss. She wasn't going to tell Max about the codex—that would be her and Ace's little secret. The less people that knew about it, the better.

If Max wanted to punish her for not finding the tomb, then so be it.

CHAPTER TWENTY-SEVEN

Five days later, Kate sat uncomfortably in the lab next to Gideon, awaiting a Skype call from Max. After the incident at the pyramid, they had gone back to their campsite and awaited the next satellite feed to talk to Gideon so Kate could give him the bad news. The subsequent instructions from Max were to pack up immediately and come home.

On the way out, they made a hasty trip to Jersey's campsite. Oddly enough, the tents were still set up but there was no sign of Ed.

The door whisked open and Kate's lips curled in distaste as Mercedes LaChance sashayed into the room. Her eyes shot daggers at Kate as she fisted her hands on her hips and demanded, "What did you do to Ace Mason?"

Kate scowled at Mercedes. Why did *she* care? As liaison between the museum and the FBI, Mercedes' job was to interface with the agents they sometimes teamed up with to recover stolen museum items. That meant that Mercedes spent a lot of time talking with Ace.

"I didn't *do* anything to him. What's wrong with him?" Kate asked.

"He got fired from the FBI."

"You're kidding, right?" Kate felt a stab of guilt. The FBI was Ace's life. If he'd been fired because he went to Mexico to help her, he'd be pretty mad. She hoped that wasn't the case because she didn't want to be responsible for Ace losing his job, even though it would be fitting since he was responsible for *her* getting fired from the FBI.

"His replacement just left my office," Mercedes said.

Kate glanced at Gideon, who shrugged. "I heard Ace got fired, too."

Kate didn't have time to think about that because just then, Gideon's computer made a ringing sound.

"That's Max calling in from Budapest." Gideon pressed a few buttons and the Skype screen appeared.

Kate fluffed her hair. She was excited to finally see her elusive boss, but also nervous to hear what he would say about her mucking up the mission.

She stared at the screen in anticipation, confusion crossing her face when all she saw were two legs sticking up.

"Hi, everybody." Max's sultry melodic voice drifted out of the computer. "I hope you don't mind if I practice some of my yoga while we are on this call. I'm pressed for time and need to try to kill two birds with one stone."

Gideon laughed. "That's okay, Max. I guess we can

talk to your feet as well as your face."

"Great," Max said. "Did you do the research I asked for?"

"Yes," Gideon said. "I found out that Jersey was working for *Teledig*. She was on a genuine dig to recover a Mayan village, but what they didn't know was that she was secretly trying to pick up where her grandfather had left off, behind the scenes."

"So, she was using the Mayan dig is a cover to try to find the tomb Reginald White claimed to have uncovered thirty years ago?" Kate asked.

Gideon nodded. "That's right. She got her expenses paid to go out there and actually was doing the work for them but also following her grandfather's footsteps on the side."

"What about her assistant, Ed?" Kate asked.

Gideon frowned. "That's the thing. They didn't send out any assistant named Ed. They'd never heard of him. Are you sure you got the name right?"

Kate bristled. What did they think—she was so unstable that she couldn't remember people's names? "Of course I did. Everyone there saw him."

"Well, it sounds like a mystery, then," Max's voice said. "But tell me, are you sure that you didn't find any sign of a tomb."

Kate's gut tingled with nerves. She hated lying to Max and Gideon but she couldn't risk telling them about the whole time travel thing. She knew instinctively that the less people that knew about it, the less chance others would try to seek it out.

"Unfortunately, there was no tomb. We found the

rest of the map and followed it explicitly, but it just led to an empty pyramid," Kate said.

"And what about my friend, Markovic?" Max asked.

"Oh, he sent his guys out there. Unfortunately, they had a run-in with Jersey and I don't think they will be bothering us again—well, at least one of them won't." Kate wondered if Onion Mole had ever dislodged the snake … or made it out of the jungle. She felt a smug satisfaction, picturing him wandering around in there lost.

"Word on the street is now that they know there's no tomb, Markovic has turned his interest to some other treasure," Gideon said.

"That's great," Max said. "We don't need him dogging us at every turn. It's hard enough work for Kate to try and recover these items on her own. In fact, I think it's too much work for her."

Kate's heart swooped. Here it comes, she thought. Failing to find the tomb was going to count against her. Would she be relegated to a desk for the rest of her career? Demoted and made to stand guard at the doors? She held her breath in anticipation of Max's next words.

Gideon shot Kate a sympathetic glance. She figured he was probably working out the same scenarios in his head that she was in hers. "What you mean by that?"

"I've decided to step up our rate of acquisition. And with more displays for the museum, that probably means we'll be seeing more theft. It's going to be too much work for one person, so I've hired a partner for you to work with, Kate."

Kate felt like she'd been punched in the gut.

A partner was worse than a desk job. She didn't work well with others and she certainly didn't need someone tagging along, who she had to train or watch out for to make sure they didn't get killed.

"Wait a minute. I can do this by myself. Another person will just slow me down. I don't need to be watching out for someone else out in the field," she begged.

"Oh, I don't think you'll have to watch out for this person. I've hired someone who is highly skilled and trained in this job. They should be able to take care of themselves," Max said.

"But…"

"Now, Kate." Max's feet wiggled on the screen. "I know you might resist this at first, but I think you're going to really be glad about this in the end. In fact, I've invited your new partner to join this meeting. They should be here at any minute. I took the liberty of giving out the code to the lab."

Kate, Gideon and Mercedes exchanged confused glances as they heard the elevator. Kate perched on the edge of her seat, anticipation mingled with trepidation as the elevator came to a stop.

Her feelings turned to horror as the door slid open to reveal her new partner was none other than *former* FBI agent Ace Mason.

———

"Why would he saddle me with Ace Mason?" Kate asked her parents two weeks later while enjoying iced tea in the outdoor cafe near their Florida condo.

Vic shrugged. "You always worked good together at the bureau."

Kate scowled at Vic over her straw. "That was before I knew he was a jerk."

"Maybe that's all part of the curse," Carlotta joked. "Just because there was no tomb doesn't mean there wasn't a curse."

"Very funny." Kate sucked a mouthful of iced tea up through her straw. She still felt bad about keeping the truth from her parents, but it was the best thing. Still, there had been a tomb, so maybe she really was being cursed.

"Anyway, I'm just glad to be away from all those mosquitos," Vic scratched a series of red welts on his arm.

"And the snakes," Kate added.

"We were very proud of how you conquered your fear of them on the pyramid. Weren't we, Vic?" Carlotta beamed a ray of parental pride at Kate that made her heart swell.

"We're always proud of you, Kitten." Vic put his large paw over Kate's hand and they all smiled at each other while the waiter placed a large blooming onion in the center of the table.

Kate's eyes were drawn to the fragrant fried appetizer, her mouth watering as she reached over to pick off one of the slabs of onion before the waiter even finished setting the tray down. As he withdrew his hand from the platter, she noticed his tattoo—a figure eight snake eating its own tail.

She jerked her head up to look at his face. Their eyes

locked and she sucked in a breath. It was the guy from the tomb!

"Hey, you're—"

But then he was gone, the back of his head disappearing in the crowd. Kate sprang up from her chair, searching the crowd for him but he wasn't within sight. She ran into the restaurant, but he wasn't there, either. He had disappeared.

On the way back to her table, she signaled a nearby waiter. "Hey, our waiter that just brought the onion, did you see where he went?"

The waiter frowned down at the blooming onion. "I'm your waiter. I'm not sure who brought this."

Kate's phone erupted in song, interrupting her search for the mysterious waiter. Her parents were looking at her strangely, after her odd reaction to the waiter. Too bad she couldn't tell them why she'd reacted like that. They probably thought she'd imagined recognizing the waiter. Maybe she had? After all, it was highly unlikely the guy would turn up here in Florida impersonating a waiter. But still, she couldn't stop her eyes from wandering around the room, looking for the tattooed wrist as she answered her phone.

"Hi, Gideon," Kate answered. She couldn't tell him about the strange man, either. But Gideon wasn't calling to chat anyway. He was calling to tell her about her next assignment.

The blood drained from Kate's face as he gave her the details.

"What is it, dear?" her mother asked after she hung up. "It's not about snakes, is it, because you conquered that fear and you don't have to worry about freezing up when you encounter them ever again."

"It's not snakes," Kate said grimly. "It's much worse than that?"

Vic and Carlotta exchanged a worried glance. "What is it?"

"It's my next assignment." Kate tore off a huge chunk of blooming onion and stuffed it in her mouth. Maybe greasy fried food would soften the blow of what Gideon had just told her.

Vic frowned. "What is it that could be so bad? Is it a boring desk job again?"

Kate shook her head.

"Going out in the field in Antarctica?" Carlotta asked, knowing the cold weather and lack of anything to do would not appeal to Kate.

"Nope."

"Recovering a stolen museum piece from an un-guarded house?" Vic knew this would be a boring, pedestrian assignment.

"No."

"Then what?" Vic and Carlotta asked at the same time.

Kate sighed and signaled the waiter to bring another drink. She needed something stronger. Much stronger.

"My next assignment involves going undercover as a married woman … married to my new partner, Ace Mason."

Want to read more of Kate's adventures?

Get the other books in the series:

Hidden Agemda (Book 1)

More books coming soon!

A NOTE FROM THE AUTHOR

Thanks so much for reading, "Ancient Hiss Story". I hope you liked reading it as much as I loved writing it. If you did, and feel inclined to leave a review, I really would appreciate it.

This is book two of the Kate Diamond adventure series. I plan to write many more books with Kate and the *Golden Capers* gang. I have several other series that I write, too - you can find out more about them on my website: *http://www.leighanndobbs.com*.

This book has been through many edits with several people and even some software programs, but since nothing is infallible (even the software programs), you might catch a spelling error or mistake and, if you do, I sure would appreciate it if you let me know - you can contact me at: *lee@leighanndobbs.com*.

Oh, and I love to connect with my readers, so please visit me on facebook at *http://www.facebook.com/leighanndobbsbooks*

Signup to get my newest releases at a discount: *http://www.leighanndobbs.com/newsletter*

If you want to receive a text message on your cell phone when I have a new release, text COZYMYSTERY to 88202. (Sorry, this only works for US cell phones!)

ABOUT THE AUTHOR

USA Today Bestselling author Leighann Dobbs has had a passion for reading since she was old enough to hold a book, but she didn't put pen to paper until much later in life. After a twenty-year career as a software engineer with a few side trips into selling antiques and making jewelry, she realized you can't make a living reading books, so she tried her hand at writing them and discovered she had a passion for that, too! She lives in New Hampshire with her husband, Bruce, their trusty Chihuahua mix, Mojo, and beautiful rescue cat, Kitty.

Find out about her latest books and how to get discounts on them by signing up at:

http://www.leighanndobbs.com/newsletter

If you want to receive a text message alert on your cell phone for new releases , text COZYMYSTERY to 88202. (Sorry, this only works for US cell phones!)

Connect with Leighann on Facebook and Twitter:

http://facebook.com/leighanndobbsbooks
http://twitter.com/leighanndobbs